MW01533071

THERAPIST

THERAPIST

Richard Alleman
&
Peter Garrett

Walker and Company
New York

First published in the United States of America in 1989 by Walker Publishing Company, Inc.

Published simultaneously in Canada by Thomas Allen & Son Canada, Limited, Markham, Ontario

Library of Congress Cataloging-in-Publication Data

Alleman, Richard.
Therapist / Richard Alleman & Peter Garrett.
p. cm.
ISBN 0-8027-5747-2
I. Garrett, Peter, 1940–   . II. Title.
PS3551.L386T48   1989
813'.54—dc20   89-36424

Printed in the United States of America

2   4   6   8   10   1   3   5   7   9

To M. E. Rich
AND
J. R. Hamil

THERAPIST

I.

August 1

The young woman screamed as she fell onto the bed and the man came down hard on top of her.

"Oh, please, no!" she pleaded. "Not again!"

Wally Darrow didn't hear her words. He heard only a high-pitched sound of terror that caused his hands to reposition themselves around the woman's pale neck. The woman's piercing screams turned into a muffled mix of coughing and gagging.

Wally squeezed even harder, and the woman's face, white with fear seconds earlier, became scarlet. Soon, the taut mass of her body gave up and went limp. It was very quiet now.

Wally let go, and the woman's head fell back onto the bed and rolled to one side. He stood up but didn't leave—he was mesmerized by the lifeless blue eyes of the woman who lay so peacefully before him. Something snapped inside his brain. For the first time, he realized that he was looking at someone he had never seen before in his life. For the first time, too, he felt afraid. He had murdered her.

She had screamed, he knew that. Someone could have, must have, heard her. Someone might be coming this very moment. He had to get out.

Wally looked around the tiny bedroom, trying desperately to figure out how he had gotten inside. On the other side of the bed, he saw a door. He leapt toward it and opened it, but it turned out to be a closet. He spun around and saw another door across the room. It had a large dead bolt on it, and Wally was sure it led outside.

Outside . . . but where?

He sprang to the door. It was unlocked, and Wally opened it slowly. The light on the other side was much brighter than in the bedroom, and he had to squint before a long hallway came into focus. There were a lot of doors. All of them were alike and each had a number.

He stuck his head further outside. The hallway was empty. At one end there was a lighted exit sign. As he ran toward it, he heard a door open and shut quickly. Had the people inside heard the woman's screams? Did they know?

Wally was now running down flights and flights of gray concrete. He had no idea what floor he'd been on. It seemed as if the stairs went on forever. When they finally ended, he found himself in a dimly lit basement full of old furniture and suitcases. He had gone too far.

He ran back up a flight of stairs and came upon a door with a small window. Through the window, he glimpsed a lobby and a uniformed man standing at a desk. Beyond the man, glass doors led to the street.

Wally stood perfectly still. He was now aware of the wailing of sirens, and he saw a police car with flashing lights pull up in front of the glass doors. Two policemen ran into the lobby, where the man behind the desk met them and whisked them into an elevator.

It was time for a move. Slowly, almost calmly, Wally opened the door, slipped past the unattended desk, and was swallowed up by the neon night of New York City.

He was running now, flying down a street that a sign said was West Forty-seventh. It was a hot night and the sidewalk was packed with tourists, theater-goers, street people. Teenagers carried gigantic radios that blared rap music. Clumps of spectators huddled around fast-talking con artists dealing Three Card Monte on stacks of cardboard boxes.

As Wally darted in and out of the crowds, all he could think about was getting as far away as possible from where he had just been . . . from what had just happened. He ran across Seventh Avenue and kept running until he reached the end of the block. He had no idea where he was going—or where he could go.

He kept running. By the time he came to the next corner, his heart was pounding and his chest ached. He turned left and managed to stagger up two more blocks. Finally, at Rockefeller Center, he collapsed on a bench. None of the strollers on Fifth Avenue seemed to notice him as he sat trying to catch his breath, trying to make sense out of the last hours. He looked up. Across the avenue loomed St. Patrick's Cathedral, its gray limestone facade floodlit for the tourists. Suddenly, looking at the great church, Wally remembered Paul.

Seeing a phone on the corner of Fiftieth Street, Wally ran to it and lifted the receiver. As he put a quarter into the slot, he looked at the cathedral, and the words of a prayer came together in his head. It was an old prayer, one he hadn't thought of in years.

Oh my God, I am sorry for all my sins,
because they displease Thee,
who art all good and deserving of all my love.
With thy help, I will sin no more.

He started to cry as he dialed Paul's number. He had faith now. He was sure that Paul would not only forgive him . . . Paul would save him.

* * *

Paul Manning sat stretched out comfortably in the large black leather reclining chair in his office. He was engrossed in the view of the Acropolis on the postcard he held in front of him. When the telephone on his desk started ringing, he flipped over the card and read its message once more before getting up to answer the call.

Darling,
Mykonos was fun—and Brad and Lucy's house is a dream. But so many tourists! Zipping through Athens (HOT!) again en route to the Peloponnesus. Fewer crowds I hear. Wish you were here—I really do. If the truth must be told, I'm a lousy solo traveler. Separate vacations aren't what they're cracked up to be. Looking forward to our week together. But hurry! Crete is waiting—and so am I. Your wife, who loves you . . . Vivian.

"Hello," Paul said calmly into the phone, putting the postcard down on his desk.

"Dr. Manning, is that you?" a frightened, trembling voice asked.

"Yes," Paul answered, recognizing Wally Darrow on the other end of the line.

"Doc, you gotta help me," Wally begged. "I'm in trouble again. I . . . I think I just killed somebody."

Paul froze, his eyes fixed on the picture of the Acropolis in front of him.

"Doc? Doc? Are you still there?" Wally was shouting hysterically.

Paul, his head now starting to throb, didn't answer.

"Doc, did you hear me? Doc, you gotta help me!"

Paul took a deep breath. Unsure as to how the words would come out, he spoke very carefully.

"I heard you, Wally. I heard you. Now, tell me about it . . . slowly."

"Doc, I was in a hotel room with this chick I never saw before—and I killed her. I don't know how. I don't know why. I just know I did it. The cops are there now. Doc, you gotta help me."

"You know I'll help you, Wally," Paul said. "But are you sure that what you're saying is the truth? Couldn't it be that you're just imagining it? You've been through a lot these last couple of weeks."

"Jesus Christ, Doc. What do you think I am? Nuts?"

Paul didn't answer.

"Well, I'm not," Wally exclaimed. "I told you, I saw her lying there. My hands were around her neck. Christ, Doc, what the fuck am I gonna do?"

"Wally, listen to me. First of all, where are you?"

"I . . . I'm at a pay phone. Fiftieth and Fifth Avenue."

"You're not far from the hospital then. I want you to get into a cab and go right over to the Emergency Room. Do you have any money?"

"Yeah, I got some. But why the hospital? Why not your place?"

"You're closer to the hospital, Wally. It will save time."

"You're not gonna lock me up or nothing, are you?"

"I'm going to help you, Wally," Paul answered. "If what you're telling me is true, you're going to need all the help you can get. If it's not, I still want to see you."

"But, Doc, can't I come down to your place? We can talk there. We always have. I hate that fucking hospital."

"No, Wally," Paul insisted. "Go to the hospital. I may want to give you something to help calm you down, and I don't have anything here."

"But—"

"I'm leaving for the hospital now, Wally. I'll meet you in the Emergency Room in about fifteen minutes. If you get there before I do, just tell the nurse that I'm on my way."

"Fuck, Doc, I'm scared. I've never been so fucking scared in my whole life."

"I know you are, Wally."

"What's gonna happen, Doc?"

"I'm going to do everything I can. Trust me."

"Thanks, Doc. Thanks."

Paul hung up the phone and stood immobile at his desk, his hand still on the receiver. He tried to collect his thoughts and go over in his mind what had to be done. It was going to be a long night, but it was the kind of night that, from time to time, a psychiatrist had to deal with.

He looked around his office, his eyes zeroing in on a lacquered cabinet that was part of a bookshelf unit spanning the back wall of the room. Taking a key out of the top desk drawer, Paul went to the cabinet and unlocked it. Inside lay a leather-bound journal from Mark Cross that Vivian had given him for his thirty-eighth birthday, nine months ago. At the time, he'd been toying with the idea of writing a book, a novel about psychiatry. He had started the journal with character sketches of some of his patients. Later, he'd turned to entering his own thoughts and dreams into the journal as well. Of course, he couldn't write a book now . . .

As Paul took the journal into the living room of his Greenwich Village townhouse, he couldn't help thinking about his young patient. Poor Wally Darrow. If he had had a little luck, perhaps he could have been the all-American boy. He certainly looked the part with his bright red hair and freckles. But something had gone wrong somewhere, and Paul knew that it was more than just a question of bad luck.

The journal didn't burn as easily as Paul had thought it would. The cover was the problem. The pages disappeared quickly enough, but the leather just smoldered and made a foul odor. When the flames died down, Paul removed the charred cover with fireplace tongs and put it in the garbage can in the kitchen. He stirred the garbage around with the tongs so that the journal cover wouldn't be at the top. Tomorrow morning the New York City Sanitation Department would take care of the rest.

July 5

Paul Manning strode into the basement room used for giving shock treatments with only one thought in mind: how much he dreaded July. It was the month when the new crop of psychiatric residents arrived at New York General Hospital. As director of residency training, Paul was responsible for shaping these young men and women—who had spent the last four years with textbooks, laboratory animals, and cadavers—into doctors who dealt with human beings with feelings and real problems.

"Good afternoon, everyone," Paul said pleasantly, and with as much confidence as he could muster to the twelve first-year residents standing near an operating table at the front of the room. He sensed that they were anxious over what was about to take place, but he had learned long ago that there was little he could do to make shock palatable.

Without another word, he began applying a colorless jelly to the right temple of an elderly woman strapped to the table. The woman's hair was pulled away from her face, and she was dressed in a white hospital gown. She was conscious but heavily anesthetized.

"Mrs. Stein has had three treatments in the last ten days," Paul explained, as he taped an electrode to the woman's temple. "Already there's been an enormous improvement in both sleep and appetite."

He indicated the tiny Taiwanese man standing quietly beside him.

"Dr. Wong, our anesthesiologist, has just administered the muscle relaxant, succinylcholine, to minimize fractures. Before that, he gave Mrs. Stein a barbiturate to cut down on the sensation of respiratory distress. The patient's dentures have been removed and, as you can see, we've got a gag in place to keep her from swallowing her tongue. The cardiogram this morning was within normal limits. All we have to do now is apply the voltage."

Paul paused and looked around at his students.

"Any questions?" he asked.

"Yes," a young woman with close-cropped black hair said rather aggressively. "Why aren't you using antidepressants instead of shock?"

"Because, Dr. Wyler," Paul responded, not surprised by a question he heard every year, "in cases of severe depression such as this, antidepressants have proved useless. When Mrs. Stein was admitted, she was mute, withdrawn, and anorectic. Furthermore, she had the delusion that both her arms were missing."

"But won't she suffer memory loss from this treatment?"

"She may—but she'll get over it. Let's not forget the severity of Mrs. Stein's illness. Considering the state she's been in, there's a very real possibility of her starving herself to death. I'm sure you'll all agree that a temporary memory loss is the lesser evil."

If Dr. Wyler was not satisfied with Paul's argument, she kept it to herself as Paul edged toward a small gray box on a rolling stand.

"Now, as you all know," Paul went on, deliberately avoiding eye contact with Dr. Wyler, "the actual electric shock lasts only a fraction of a second. All we do is induce a seizure by means of the current."

He raised his hand and placed it on a black switch on the control box.

"This is the button," Paul said, aware of the silent tension that had come over the group. "Now, we just press—"

"No, don't!" a voice blurted out. Again, it was Dr. Wyler.

"This is inhuman! I can't believe that you're still doing this kind of thing. It's barbaric!"

Paul looked at her sternly, realizing as he began to talk that he was angry—not only with Wyler, but with himself for being on the brink of losing control.

"I'd like to point out to you," he said in a low voice, trying very hard to keep his feelings in check, "that none of you—nor myself for that matter—is here to pass judgment on the therapeutic policies or practices of this hospital. You are here to learn as much as you can about psychiatric medicine. ECT is a fact of life in our profession. No matter how any of us feels about it, we're going to have to face its reality, if we're going to practice psychiatry. Granted, the technique does appear crude. However, it happens to be a technique that, in many instances, works. So until someone comes up with something better, ECT is going to be with us. No matter how inhuman or barbaric we think it is."

As he spoke, Paul was aware of the sweat that had formed on his forehead and that was now dripping down into his eyes. He had let the girl get to him—and he was sure the whole class realized it.

"If you like," he went on, wiping his forehead with a handkerchief, "you can look at it as a last-resort therapy—something you use when all else fails. It's also something that, when you are practicing psychiatrists, you can choose not to use."

He directed this at Dr. Wyler, but the young woman had long since turned her face away from Paul and was now staring at the green and white tiles of the linoleum floor.

"Let me emphasize," Paul said, returning his attention to the rest of the group, "that whether or not you use ECT is not the issue here today. This is a class—a demonstration. So let's get on with it."

Before anyone could respond, Paul engaged the switch. At first, nothing seemed to happen. After a few seconds, however, the woman on the table gave a low moan as her arms and neck started to twitch. The twitching became more and more intense until, finally, her whole body was writhing violently. In fifteen seconds, the convulsion stopped, and Mrs. Stein lay peacefully on the table.

Paul turned to Dr. Wong and nodded. The anesthesiologist nodded back, then checked to see that the patient was breathing without difficulty.

"She'll come to in five minutes or so," Paul told his students, as the Chinese doctor started wheeling the woman out of the room with the help of an attendant. "She'll be confused, she may have a headache, but as I said, these symptoms will pass. Any more questions?"

The group was silent.

Relieved that the session was over, Paul dismissed the class. His watch showed that he had forty minutes before his squash game. That would give him enough time to drop in on Max.

* * *

Paul stepped out of the elevator on the sixth floor of the hospital and headed down a green hallway much in need of paint. As he reached a private room off by itself at the end of the corridor, a young woman with long brown hair and deep blue eyes was leaving. She wore jeans and a T-shirt, and to Paul, she looked attractive in a waiflike way. He smiled at her as he started to enter the room, but before he could open the door, the young woman stopped him.

"Oh, you mustn't. Not now. They just made me leave."

Paul turned and gave her a quizzical look.

"You're here to see Dr. Abrams?" she asked.

Paul nodded.

"Well, you see, they're doing something to him now," she explained. "Removing some fluid or something like that."

"I see," Paul said, realizing that his friend was probably having fluid drawn out of his pulmonary cavity—a common procedure to help advanced cancer patients breathe.

"They asked me to leave," the woman continued to explain.

"Well, I'm a doctor," Paul said with a sympathetic smile. "Perhaps they'll be a little less strict with me."

"Oh, I'm sorry. I didn't realize."

"It's all right. How is he, by the way?"

She looked at Paul with the large eyes of a child.

"I don't know why Dr. Abrams has to suffer so much. I don't know why anybody has to suffer like that."

"I'm afraid I don't have the answer to that question," Paul said gently.

"He could barely talk today. He was in such pain, and there was nothing I could do to help him."

"He'll feel better once they drain that fluid."

"I hope so," she sighed. "He's such a good person."

"Are you a relative of his?" Paul asked. "I haven't seen you here before."

"No," she replied hesitantly, as a resident and a nurse came out of Dr. Abrams's room. "Just a friend."

Paul turned to the resident.

"How's he doing?"

The resident shrugged his shoulders noncommittally.

"Is he up for a visit?" Paul asked.

"Sure, he's awake," the resident replied before continuing on his rounds with the nurse.

"Do you want to go back inside?" Paul asked the young woman.

"I think I should be going. Just tell him Joanna said good-bye."

"I'll do that, Joanna," Paul said, and slipped quietly into the room.

Max Abrams, chairman of New York General's Psychiatry Department for the last twelve years, lay on a hospital bed that had been adjusted to almost a sitting position. A plastic pouch of clear liquid hung upside down from a pole at the head of the bed, and a tube ending in a needle led from the bottle's neck to Max's bone-thin left forearm. Another tube ran from an oxygen outlet on the wall behind the bed to Max's nose, where it was taped. Max's face was ashen. His eyes, set back deep in their sockets, were wide open, but showed little sign of life.

Paul approached the bed, not sure if Max was conscious of his presence in the room.

was here earlier," Max said, his voice
nly businesslike as he spoke of Alec
airman of the board of directors of the

—... raul said, trying to sound casual.

"I put in a good word for you."

"Thanks—but what do you mean?"

"Doctor, don't play innocent with me. Somebody's going to have to replace this worn-out department chairman here, and you know damn well I'd like
it to be you."

"That's nice of you, Max."

"Nice, nothing. You deserve it. But Graham isn't
quite as sure as I am. Seems he and a couple of other
board members think you're a little young for the job,
Paul."

"But who else is there?" Paul asked, hoping he
didn't sound too upset.

"Nobody in this hospital. But there's a big world
out there, and a lot of psychiatrists would like nothing
better than to have my job. Anyhow, getting back to
you, it seems that there's more to Graham's reserva-
tions about you than just your age. He told me he's not
sure how easygoing you are."

"Easygoing! In this madhouse! Come on now,
Max. What are you saying?"

"I'm saying that maybe Graham has a point. Just
look at you now. You seem overwrought, tired, excit-
able. You also look like you didn't sleep so hot last
night. What's the matter, Paul?"

"Max, I've just come from playing executioner
before twelve first-year residents. How do you want me
to look?"

"That's just the point, Paul. You take everything so seriously. Lighten up a little. Relax! You know, the trouble with you is that you're so busy being super-psychiatrist you don't realize that there's a whole other side to the workings of the hospital."

"What do you mean?"

"Let me ask you something. There was a fund-raising cocktail party for the new wing last week. I hear through the grapevine that you didn't show. How come?"

"I had a private patient, a guy who comes down here all the way from Poughkeepsie. I couldn't cancel on him."

"You should have, Paul. I mean, I understand why you didn't. But Graham and the rest of the board don't. Ninety percent of being a department chairman is public relations. If you want the job, you've got to attend every hospital function, and you've got to really turn on the charm, because the board members want to see how you'll represent the hospital to the outside world. And while we're on the subject of your future, let me give you another word to the wise."

"What's that?"

"Go easy on your residents. If they've got any complaints this year, they won't have me to come to. That means they could go right to Graham. We all know that you can come on a little strong at times when you're teaching."

"They've got to learn the facts of life."

"Sure they do. And you do a good job of teaching them. All I'm saying is that if any of them have any problems, you wouldn't want Graham finding out about it . . . especially at this time."

"I understand," Paul said, wondering if he had already blown it with his lecture on shock.

"Between us, I think you'll get the job. I'm only pointing out possible problem areas. Like I always do."

Max looked at his protégé warmly before changing the subject.

"How's Vivian?"

"Couldn't be better," Paul answered. "She's off to the Greek Islands tomorrow."

"Alone?"

"I think so," Paul said jokingly.

"You're the one who needs the vacation, Dr. Manning."

"I'm joining her there next month."

"That's nice. You know, Eva and I were supposed to go to Greece once. We had it all planned. We were going to take a cruise . . . Greece, Israel, Turkey. Then she got sick and . . . " His voice drifted off and Paul could see tears welling up in the old man's sunken, glazed eyes. Max's wife had died three years ago, and he had never gotten over it.

"I'm glad she's gone," Max went on, his voice now so weak that Paul could barely hear him. "I mean, I wouldn't want her to see me . . . like this."

He started to cough, and then, to retch.

"Oh, Christ!" Max said between gasps. "It hurts so goddamned much! Why, in God's name? Why does it have to end like this?"

"Max, let me get the nurse to give you a shot," Paul said, turning around and heading out into the corridor.

As he walked down the hallway, he could feel his stomach churning. By the time he reached the nurses' station, Paul realized that, ultimately, he agreed with Max Abrams. He didn't know why it had to end like this either.

Already late for his squash match, Paul decided to take a shortcut through the psychiatric Emergency Room. A mistake. As he glanced through the windowed doors into the patient holding area, he saw a short, stocky, red-haired man standing on top of the admissions desk and urinating into a wastebasket below. Marge Kaplan, the nurse on duty, was trying to pull the man down with the aid of a policeman. Paul kissed his squash game good-bye and entered the room.

"Let me fucking piss, goddamn it! Let me piss in peace!" the young man bellowed.

Marge saw Paul and looked relieved.

"Thank God, Doctor Manning. We've got a real tune on our hands, I'm afraid."

"What's the problem?"

"Officer Johnson just brought him in off the street. Drunk out of his skull. Evidently he was exposing himself to pedestrians."

"Let me have five milligrams of Haldol."

Marge rushed to a cabinet at the far end of the room and started filling a syringe.

"Who the fuck are you?" the man demanded belligerently when Paul approached him. He had stopped urinating by now.

"Button up your fly," Paul said. "This is a hospital, not a rest room."

"I told them I had to take a leak. Can I help it if they wouldn't let me?"

"I had him handcuffed," the policeman explained

to Paul, as the two of them grabbed the man and pulled him off the desk. "But when I took them off him so he could sign the admittance forms, all hell broke loose."

"Let go of me," the man screamed, as he was forced to the floor and handcuffed again. He looked up and saw Marge hand a large syringe to Paul, along with an alcohol-soaked cotton ball.

"Stay away from me with that fucking thing!"

"Keep him still, officer," Paul said to the cop. He rubbed the patient's upper arm with the cotton and smoothly jabbed in the hypodermic.

"You sons of bitches!" the man wailed.

"That should quiet him," Paul said.

"All you bastards know how to do is shoot people up and turn 'em into zombies. I know all about you fucking people."

"Better put him in the Quiet Room, Marge," Paul instructed calmly.

"What the fuck's a Quiet Room?"

"It's where you're going to get some rest," Paul answered. "Then, someone will see you."

"I don't want to see anybody. I just want to get the fuck out of here."

"You'll be able to go after you settle down." Paul turned to Marge and spoke to her in a low voice. "Be sure to check his pockets. We don't want him to be able to hurt himself."

"Should we leave the handcuffs on?" the nurse asked.

"No, you can take them off," Paul replied. "He'll be all right in there."

Marge followed Officer Johnson, who had already started dragging the young man across the floor of the

Emergency Room toward the padded Quiet Room reserved for violent cases.

Paul looked at the clock on the wall and realized that he should call the Harvard Club and let his squash partner know that he wasn't going to be there after all. Roy Bradley wouldn't mind, since it was easy to pick up a game around five o'clock. In fact, he was probably playing with someone else already. Paul minded. He hadn't bothered to jog that morning, and now, he would wind up the day with practically no exercise.

Paul called the club, left his message, and hung up. He was about to check on how Marge and the policeman were doing when he looked up and saw an extremely tall woman with long, platinum blonde hair standing before him. She wore a black sheath dress from the early 1950s, ankle-strap high-heeled shoes, and bright red lipstick.

"Hi, guy!" she addressed Paul familiarly. "Up for some fun?"

"Sorry, Connie, not this afternoon," Paul answered briskly. He remembered having seen the woman several weeks ago when she had had a bad reaction to some crack. He also remembered that the bizarre-looking blonde was actually a man.

"Oh shit, Doctor. You're no fun at all. I bet you wouldn't even give a girl who's got the worst headache in town a nice big shot of Demerol either, would you?"

"Has anybody seen you yet?"

"No, honey. I just got here."

"Well, when it's your turn, I'm sure you'll get the medication you need, if any."

"But I want Demerol, darling! Demerol! Connie's got a headache. Don't you understand?"

"Just take a seat," Paul said, leading her by the hand to one of the benches. "We'll take good care of you."

Suddenly, the big drag queen was all Southern charm.

"Oh, Doctor, you do know how to treat a lady. A good man is so hard to find these days. Especially for a girl like I."

Paul smiled faintly as Marge and Johnson reentered the room.

"Thank God you wandered by when you did, Paul," Marge said. "The resident on duty went home for the day. Got sick to his stomach while seeing a guy who'd tried suicide, a jumper. The replacement hasn't arrived yet. We've had our hands full."

"All in a day's work," Paul observed with a resigned shrug, trying to ignore Connie, who was now blowing him kisses from across the room. "How's our friend in the Quiet Room doing?"

"Still pretty agitated. I wish you'd see him."

"That guy must have been drinking the last twenty-four hours," Johnson put in. "Guess he's still celebrating the Fourth!"

"Good thing you got him to us when you did," Paul said. "You did a good job."

"Like you said, Doc. All in a day's work." The policeman started out of the room. "God knows how many other nuts I'll run into before the night is over," he added before disappearing out the doors.

Paul waved to the officer, said good-bye to Marge, and headed toward the Quiet Room. Midway down the corridor, he stopped at a water fountain and took a small gold pillbox out of his pocket. He opened it and looked thoughtfully at the pale blue ten-milligram tablets of Valium inside. He had begun feeling edgy since the shock session with the residents. Seeing Max had added to his uneasiness. Then the young alcoholic. Tomorrow, Vivian would be leaving for Greece. This would be their last night together.

Paul continued to stare at the tablets, wondering whether to take all of one, or just half. He decided on half. No use rushing things. He could always take the other half later.

The young man who had been so disorderly a few minutes ago was now sleeping soundly, snoring loudly on one of the four cots that lined the Quiet Room's padded walls. There was no other furniture.

Paul walked over to his patient, repelled by the smell coming from the man's filthy clothing, and tried rousing him by shaking his shoulders. Getting no response, Paul slapped him lightly on the side of his face. Still the man didn't budge. Paul slapped him a little harder.

"Wake up, I want to talk to you," he said.

The man continued to sleep. Paul grabbed a fold of skin on the young man's neck with his thumb and forefinger and pinched. Gently at first, then harder. The man gave a start and sat up.

"Jesus Christ . . . what the fuck?" he said, dazed, clutching his neck.

"I wanted to see you before I left," Paul said, sitting down on the next cot.

"I don't have anything to say," The young man blinked his eyes and lay down again.

"Don't," Paul warned. "Not yet."

"But I feel like shit."

"I'm sure you do," Paul agreed. He held out a cup of water he'd brought from the water fountain. "Here."

The man looked at it and slowly rose, extending his arm. It was a difficult maneuver, but he managed to pull it off. He gulped down the water in one swallow.

"What's your name?" Paul asked.

"Why do you care?"

"If we're going to be talking to one another, it's easier to use first names. Mine's Paul. Paul Manning."

"Wally Darrow."

"How old are you?"

"Twenty-seven."

"What do you usually drink?"

"I'm not choosy."

"What were you drinking today?"

"Don't remember. Started with gin, I think."

"Been drinking for long?"

"Six or seven years," Wally muttered. "'Since the Marines."

"Ever had the d.t.'s?"

"You mean like when you got bugs crawling down your throat and all that?"

Paul nodded.

"Shit, no, man."

"What about cirrhosis?"

"What about it?"

"Is your liver okay?"

"How the fuck do I know?"

"I'd bet there's a good chance it isn't," Paul said carefully, keeping any hint of judgment out of his voice.

"So what? I'll drop dead that much sooner."

"Where were you in the service?"

"All over the place. Pendleton, Camp Le Jeune, and then the real craphole."

"Which was?"

"A poor excuse for a country—Lebanon."

"What were you doing there?"

"Supposedly trying to keep the peace," he answered bitterly. "What a joke!"

"Why do you say that?"

"What the fuck is this? Twenty questions?"

"I'm here to help you."

"You can help me by leaving me alone. I don't want to think about it."

"But you can't stop thinking about it, can you?" Paul persisted gently.

"The booze lets me forget."

"It screws up your head, too."

All of a sudden, Wally sat up again.

"Look, Mr. . . . . Doctor . . . "

"Paul."

"Why don't you stop wasting your time? It's too late. You know what I mean?"

Paul got up from the cot.

"It's only too late, Wally, if you let it be."

"That's my business."

"Yes. I suppose it is." Paul started for the door.

"Hey, where the fuck are you going?"

"Back outside. You can sleep it off in here for a while longer."

"And then what?"

"And then?" Paul was matter-of-fact. "Nothing. You're free to go."

"You mean you're not gonna put me in the loony bin?"

"Look, you need help, but until you decide that for yourself, there's no way we can force you to get it. Now, if you like, I'll make an appointment for you to see someone in the clinic here."

"Clinics, shit! That's where those assholes in the Marines sent me before they drummed me out. You know what it was like? I went into this clown's office, and he must have had a hundred chairs in there and a piece of junk he called a desk. Nothing else. No pictures on the wall, nothing. So I ask him where he wants me to sit. And you know what the fuck he says? He says, 'Why do you ask?' I mean, why the fuck else was I asking with all those chairs in the goddamned room? I should have walked out right then."

"Maybe you should have."

"Then it got worse," Wally went on. "We stared at each other for like ten minutes. I didn't say anything and he didn't either. Shit, here I've just come from getting shot at by fucking Arab fanatics, and here's this jerk that's getting paid to act like a mummy. Finally, he closes his eyes, and next thing I know, the son of a bitch is snoring! Bastard didn't even wake up when I split."

"You know, it doesn't always have to be like that."

Wally snickered. "Shrinks are for people who don't know what else to do with their dough."

"Well, you know where we are if you change your mind."

"Don't hold your breath," Wally mumbled as he turned onto his stomach and stared at the gray padded wall.

Paul left quietly. He had done his professional duty. Wally Darrow would be discharged in a few hours, probably get himself into more trouble, maybe even get himself killed. But no matter what happened, Paul realized that Wally was out of anyone's reach at the moment. Alcoholics were very difficult patients—too stubborn, too self-pitying, too hostile.

He walked outside the hospital, hailed a cab, and told the driver to head for MacDougal Street in Greenwich Village. Paul sank back into the seat as the cab crept down Ninth Avenue, which was clogged with late afternoon traffic bound for the Lincoln Tunnel. At first, he couldn't figure out why, despite the traffic, he felt so tranquil. Then he realized that the Valium was kicking in.

Wally tried to piece together the fragments of the last twenty-four hours as he stood in line in front of Window 19 at the Port Authority Bus Terminal. He vaguely remembered wandering out of a hospital in the West Forties and walking toward Eighth Avenue. It was a hot, muggy July evening, and just taking a breath was an effort. He had thought of stopping at a bar on Forty-second Street, but something inside his system rejected the idea. All he wanted to do now was make it back to his room and get some sleep.

Slowly, more of the afternoon started coming back to him. There had been a lot of booze, a fight, a cop, the hospital, a nurse, and a doctor who had given him a shot with a huge needle. There had been a room with no furniture. Now there was the stifling heat of the city, made worse by all the people crowding around him.

"Hey, mister! Move up, will ya?"

An asshole at the back of the line was making

trouble. Too many assholes in the city. Too many assholes everywhere.

"Are you gonna move up or what?" someone else was whining now.

Wally wondered why he had to put up with all the noise, the people, the heat.

"Look, mister, if you're not gonna buy a ticket, you shouldn't be on line."

A ticket. Wally remembered why he was standing there. He reached for his wallet and took several steps toward the window.

"Passaic," he said, putting a ten-dollar bill on the counter.

"One way or round trip?"

"One way."

"Platform 223, Upper Level."

Wally stuffed the change into his pocket and shuffled away from the ticket window toward the center of the teeming station.

Assholes everywhere, he thought, as he pushed his way onto a crowded escalator. Now the escalator was making him nauseous. He had to get out of the terminal. He had to get out of the city, away from the assholes. He had to get home, to bed.

Another escalator took him to Platform 223, where people stood single-file, waiting to board the bus. Why did everything take so long? Why was everything so goddamned complicated? Why couldn't he just get on the bus and go home? Lines, escalators, buses, assholes—but worst of all was the air. He wasn't sure how much longer he'd be able to breathe. He began to shake.

The line moved slowly. By the time Wally was

stuffed on board the second bus, all of the seats had been taken. He clutched the overhead luggage rack, trying to keep his balance as businessmen carrying briefcases piled on. Couldn't they see that the fucking bus was full?

The air in the bus was even worse than it had been outside, and now Wally was concentrating on every breath he took, trying very hard not to throw up. He decided to get off while there was still time. But suddenly, the engine roared and the overloaded vehicle pulled out of its slot and started winding down the series of ramps. Round and round. Down and down. Wally could feel himself getting more and more dizzy by the moment.

In a minute or so, they were in the tunnel. Wally remembered how, when he was a little boy, he would drive from Jersey with his parents and two older brothers, to visit his grandfather in Brooklyn. They would take the tunnel, and it had always frightened him. What would happen if the river above got too heavy for the thing? Sometimes he got so scared that he would cry, and his brothers would make fun of him and call him a crybaby. Later, he learned not to cry, but the fear was always there.

About a quarter of the way into the tunnel, the bus stopped dead. Why weren't they moving? It was harder to breathe than ever. If he could just get to a window and open it, maybe he could get some air. Starting to gag, he reached across the teenage girl and the businessman in the seats next to him.

"Hey, what are you doing? You can't open that."

"Air . . . I gotta get some air." Wally choked out the words, trying desperately to open the window.

"Leave it alone! It's sealed shut."

If Wally couldn't get the window open, there was no doubt in his mind what would happen. He would die. With all the strength he could muster, he pushed against the panel of glass, but the window wouldn't budge. Seething with anger and frustration, Wally raised his arm and smashed the window with his fist, turning it into a web of crystal splinters. Blood poured from his hand and wrist and dripped onto the businessman's blue seersucker suit.

"What the hell's the matter with you? Are you crazy?" the man shouted, trying to shove Wally back into the aisle.

People on the bus began screaming as Wally spun around and punched at another window with his bloody fist. Somebody grabbed him and threw him to the floor. He tried to stand up, but there were too many people in the aisle. Desperate for air, he crawled along the floor to the front of the bus and managed to get to his feet.

"Gotta get out! I gotta get the fuck outta here!" Wally cried to the driver as he lunged at the door and pounded against the glass panels. Unable to break the glass with his fist, he raised his foot and kicked frantically at the bottom of the door.

"Gotta get out! Let me out!"

"Let him out! He's crazy!"

"Get him off the bus before he kills somebody!"

"For God's sake, open the door!"

Finally, the doors parted and Wally tumbled off the bus into the amber haze of the tunnel. He gasped for breath and tore open his shirt in an attempt to get air into his lungs. Cars blew their horns as he staggered in and out of the stalled traffic. Why were they all honking at him? All he wanted to do was breathe. He didn't want to die.

Paul had just finished supper and was sitting on the patio of his Greenwich Village townhouse. Looking out at the large central garden that his house shared with the others on the block, he thought about how living in "the Garden," as the block was called, was not like living in New York City at all. Here, in this enclave of privilege and serenity, people often left their back doors unlocked, neighbors visited freely with one another, and, best of all, children could grow up and play in a safe place. As he sipped a glass of straight Stolichnaya vodka over ice, Paul realized once again that, had it not been for this very special living situation, he and his family would have moved to the suburbs long ago. At the same time, serenity and safety had their price: a huge mortgage, private schools for Sean and Sarah, summer camp, the constant repair bills that came with owning and maintaining a hundred-year-old property.

A bit of a breeze had finally come up, after three very hot days and nights. Vivian Manning, wearing shorts and a tennis shirt, her hair newly highlighted and cut in a short style that Paul wasn't sure he liked, came out onto the patio to join her husband. With her was a large woman in her early fifties, dressed in a loose-fitting red caftan. Elena Rothman lived three houses down and had dropped over to say good-bye to Vivian.

"Of course, you realize, darling," Elena's deep, New York–accented voice oozed, "your trip is the envy of the garden! I mean, everybody talks about taking separate vacations, but here you are actually doing it."

"But if Paul's joining me for the last part, does it still count?" Vivian argued playfully. "It's not quite so fashionable then, is it?"

"Well, I still think it's divine," Elena replied. "And so liberated of you, Paulie!"

"It's really more a question of timing than anything else," Paul said. "Viv's wanted to go to Greece for years. With the kids at camp, and me tied up teaching at the hospital, this is a good time for her to do it."

"But all those gorgeous Greek men!" Elena's eyes twinkled mischievously. "If I were a man, I wouldn't dream of letting my wife near them. Especially now that you're so blonde, Vivian! Darling, you're positively going to have to fight them off."

"Then fight I shall, because all I'm interested in is seeing a few ruins and getting a lot of sea and sunshine," Vivian said. "Now, can I get anybody another drink?"

"Sure, honey. A short one would be great."

"Elena?" Vivian asked.

"Oh, no," she answered. "I just wanted to wish you a heavenly trip, that's all. I'm sure you have masses of things to do before tomorrow morning."

"That's sweet of you," Vivian said, walking Elena to the gate that led to the main garden. "I'll count on you to keep Paul out of trouble while I'm gone."

"I think he can more than take care of himself," Elena said, winking at Paul before she floated back toward her house.

Paul waved good-bye, but was glad to see her go. A little of Elena went a long way.

"If I didn't know better, I'd say that Madame R. has her eye on you, sweetheart," Vivian joked as she returned to where Paul was sitting.

"What happened to that kid from NYU?" Paul asked.

"Oh, that was over ages ago. The latest is someone from her Weight Watchers group."

Paul smiled. "You don't have a thing to worry about," he said, taking Vivian's hand and squeezing it. "Elena's not my type. But what about all those Greeks she's talking about?"

Vivian blushed. "Not my type either, I'm afraid. I prefer blonds." She leaned over and kissed her husband on the forehead. "I'm really going to miss you," she said softly.

Suddenly, Paul stood up, pulled his wife to him, and kissed her. It was an awkward move and it caught her by surprise.

"Let's . . . let's go to bed."

"But—"

"No buts. Let's go upstairs."

There was an urgency in his voice and in his eyes that Vivian hadn't seen for a long time. For an instant, he reminded her of a little boy.

"Are you sure you want to?"

Paul nodded.

"Yes, I'm sure," he whispered. "Tonight I'm sure."

Paul locked up the house, turned off the lights on the first floor, and climbed the stairs. When he reached the third floor, he found his wife in their daughter's room, rearranging the contents of an open suitcase that lay on a child's canopied bed.

"What are you doing?" he asked from the doorway. "Still packing?"

"It never ends." Vivian smiled, looking up from the suitcase. "I realized coming up the stairs that I'd forgotten my favorite bathing suit."

"Can't you finish tomorrow?"

"Finished!" Vivian replied, closing the valise with a flourish.

Paul switched off the light.

"Darling, I'm coming as fast as I can," Vivian kidded in the half-darkness.

"No, don't!" Paul ordered, suddenly intrigued by the sight of his wife standing next to the small white bed.

"Don't what?" Vivian asked.

"Stay there for a second. I . . . I like you there." Slowly, he moved toward her, tripping over a flight bag along the way.

"No, Paul," she protested gently. "Not here. Not in Sarah's room."

"Why not?"

"Because," Vivian answered, breaking free of her husband and walking toward the hallway. "I'd feel funny about it, that's all."

"Okay, if you say so," he responded, following her out of the room.

Vivian entered their bedroom and started undressing. Paul walked over to her, put his hands round her slim waist, and kissed her again.

"Oh, darling, I want you so much tonight," she said, grasping his arms as he lifted her and carried her to the bed.

"I want you, too," he answered. He pulled back the top sheet.

Vivian stretched out her legs and gave him a seductive look.

"Come here, you beautiful blond hunk. I want to undress you."

Paul eased down onto the bed next to her and she proceeded to remove his shirt and kiss his chest. Next she took off his Topsiders, and began sensuously massaging his feet. He grinned down at her.

She moved back up his body and undid his belt and unzipped his fly. He raised up his buttocks to help her get the pants off. She started to remove his shorts too, but he sat up, swung away from her, and took them off himself.

Turning back to her, he bent down and kissed her breasts.

"Oh, Paul, I love it when you do that," she sighed, moving her hand down his torso and hips.

"Not yet," he said, taking her hand and putting her delicate fingers in his mouth.

"It's been so long," she whispered.

Paul's mouth worked its way down her body. "Oh, God," he said. "I want you tonight. I want you so badly."

He raised his head and looked at her. His blond hair fell across his forehead, like a little boy's.

Vivian drew his face to hers and kissed him as hard as she could.

"Darling, you're so beautiful. I love you so much," she murmured. "Make love to me. Oh, please, make love to me."

Again her hand reached down. Abruptly he turned away from her.

"Paul, what is it?" she asked.

"I . . . I don't know."

"I thought you wanted to."

There was a long silence.

"I'm sorry," he said at last.

"Please let me help," she said, trying to mask her frustration. "We can try again."

"No, it's no use. Not tonight anyway. I'll be better in Greece, I promise you."

She kissed him on the cheek. "It's all right, darling," she replied. "I understand."

But as Vivian turned away and pulled the sheet up over her, Paul knew that she didn't understand at all. How could she? He didn't understand either. He hadn't understood for months.

Vivian had been asleep for almost an hour when Paul, still wide-awake, finally got out of bed and went into the bathroom. He opened the medicine chest and eyed a small plastic vial of sleeping pills. It was too early to take a Seconal, he decided. Besides, he didn't like the hangover the drug gave him the next morning. His eye moved from the sleeping pills to a container of Valium. He decided to take the Valium first, and move on to the Seconals if he weren't asleep in an hour.

As he swallowed the pill, Paul caught a glimpse of his naked body in the full-length mirror on the bathroom door. His stomach bothered him. It wasn't flabby, but it wasn't firm either. He stepped on the scale. One hundred seventy pounds. Five pounds more than he liked to weigh. Two pounds more than he had weighed at the beginning of the week. As he headed back to the bedroom, he thought of his missed squash game that afternoon. It had been almost a week since he had exercised at all, and it scared him. Another sign of losing control of things.

Paul looked at his wife lying in bed. He didn't understand how anyone could sleep so soundly. His head felt tight, and he was conscious of the blood throbbing inside it. He knew that getting back into bed now would be a waste of time, since it would be at least a half hour before the Valium would start working.

He slipped on his shorts and went downstairs to his office on the first floor. It had been a long time since he'd written anything in his journal, and as he unlocked the cabinet where he kept it, he was filled with a sense of relief. He took a pen from his desk, stretched out in the black leather chair, and started to write.

Can't sleep. Rotten day. Never should have gone to see Max. Give him three weeks at the most. So useless. Why not just let him die? The business with Vivian continues. Two months and counting. She's being good about it. I guess. But how long will she buy my being "under pressure"? Or does she think there's someone else? Hell of a note for her to leave on. But why is she going to Greece ahead of me? Kicks!!!

Really thought I'd pull it off tonight. If we had stayed in Sarah's room? For some reason, I was really hot to do it in there. Damn Vivian. Always has to have her own way. Should have made her make love where I wanted. Instead she makes me fail. Again. I hate the humiliation. Hate the way it makes me feel about her.

12:18. Head buzzing. Valium letting me down. Wonder how many patients I'd lose if they knew how helpless their therapist feels tonight? The great hoax. They come to us for miracles. Sometimes we even convince them they've made progress. Nobody suspects the truth. It's the blind leading the blind . . .

Paul put down his pen and looked over at the telephone ringing on his desk. Curious as to who could be calling him at this hour, he went over to the phone and turned up the volume control of the answering machine.

"This is Dr. Manning on a recorded announcement. I am not able to speak with you now, but if you please leave your name, telephone number, and the time that you called at the sound of the signal, I'll get back to you as soon as I can."

A beep tone sounded, and Paul heard a man's voice.

"Uh . . . Dr. Manning, this is Wally Darrow . . . from this afternoon. I . . . I don't know if you remember me or not, but . . . well, I had a real rough time of things tonight, and I think I'd better see you after all. Anyway, I'll call you back in—"

Paul picked up the receiver. "Hello, this is Dr. Manning." He wasn't sure if it was guilt or loneliness that was making him speak to the young man just now.

"Doc? I . . . I didn't think you were in. I got your number out of the phone book. This is Wally Darrow . . . the guy from this afternoon . . . "

"I remember. What can I do for you?"

"Well, Doc, I was thinking . . . about what you said this afternoon at the hospital. You know, about how you got to realize when you need help? And . . . well, I think I could use some."

"I see," Paul answered, now having second thoughts about the phone call. He hoped Wally's problem wouldn't keep him up all night.

"Yeah, you said that you'd like to help me, Doc. I remember."

[40]

"Would you like me to arrange for you to see someone at the clinic in the morning?" Paul asked.

"Clinic? No, I want to see you. You sounded—I don't know . . . different. Not like those jerks I saw in the Marines."

"Wally, look, I'd like to help you. I really would—but I have a very busy schedule. Now, if you feel this is an emergency, you can go back to the hospital emergency room tonight if you like."

"Are you telling me to forget it?" Wally asked, desperation entering his voice.

"Okay, listen. Why don't you drop by the clinic tomorrow? I'll see what I can do."

"What clinic?"

"The psychiatric clinic at New York General. On the third floor. Tell the woman at the desk that you want to make an appointment with me. We'll work something out."

"Sure, Doc. Anything you say. I'll be there."

Wally would have gone on talking, but Paul said good-bye and hung up so quickly that he didn't have the chance. Paul switched the answering machine back on and turned off the volume control. He looked down at his journal.

The great hoax. They come to us for miracles. Sometimes we even convince them they've made progress. Nobody suspects the truth. It's the blind leading the blind . . .

July 9

"The thing is, I didn't do all that much drinking before the Marines. Drugs, yes. But the booze more or less started when I got back to the States."

Wally Darrow was sitting forward in the high-backed, black leather chair in Paul's townhouse office. As he spoke, he tightly held the arm of the chair with his left hand. His right hand was bandaged.

"What made you start drinking?"

"How should I know? I mean, isn't that your job, Doc?"

Paul smiled. "Perhaps we should look on it as our job. Now, what can you tell me, Wally?"

"About drinking?"

"About anything. We've got to start somewhere."

Wally sat back slightly, his left hand still gripping the chair.

"Well, you know, I come back to the States from fucking Lebanon. I've got this funny-paper discharge ... unsuitable for military service. So I go home to my folks in Jersey, and they have this big homecoming dinner and all. But after that, that's it. It's like they don't even give a damn I'm back."

"Why do you say that?"

"I could just tell. My old man, no matter what he said on the outside, what he was really thinking was that I fucked up again."

"Are you sure he felt that way?"

"Am I sure he felt that way?"

"Yes."

Wally paused and thought. "Well, maybe we both did."

"Why did you go into the Marines, Wally?"

"Beats me. I must have been out of my mind. It was a year after I got out of high school. I wasn't exactly what you'd call a student or anything. Anyway, I got this job working in a service station over in Jersey City. I always liked cars. And then I said to myself, 'Shit, I'm not making any money here, and who wants to pump gas into somebody else's Cadillac for the rest of their life?' So I figured, what the fuck, I'd sign up."

"No other reasons, Wally?"

"That's all I can think of, Doc."

Paul looked hard at Wally, but said nothing. Wally, uncomfortable under Paul's gaze, shifted his position in the chair, then shifted again.

"Why are you looking at me like that?" he asked eventually.

"Like what?" Paul answered innocently.

"Like I should say something else."

"Do you have anything else to say?"

Wally began fiddling with the bandage on his right hand. "Shit, I don't know," he said finally. "All that 'Be a man in the United States Marines' bullshit. I guess maybe I went in to . . . to show my folks I could do something."

"They didn't think you could?"

"Look, they were old when I came along. My brother Mike is twelve years older than me, and Danny's ten years older. I just sort of showed up at the tail end of things, if you know what I mean. I mean, why should they give a shit about me?"

"You're their son."

"I was their mistake," Wally said without emotion.

"Mistake?"

"Well, they never said it, but you don't have to be too smart to realize that when a kid pops along all of a sudden after ten years, somebody fucked up somewhere. Besides, they didn't use rubbers or anything. Good Irish Catholics! My old man probably just left it in too long one night when he had no business being in there in the first place."

"Did your parents ever do anything that made you feel they didn't want you?"

"Not really."

"Then, why do you feel that way?"

"Well, my old man, I mean he never had nothing to say to me. He used to just come home after work and read the paper and eat dinner. With my brothers he could at least talk about football and sports and all that bullshit. They were in high school already and were playing on all the teams. My old man got off on that. But I was six years old. I mean, what would he talk to me about anyway?"

"What do you think he talked about to your brothers, when they were six years old?"

Wally looked up and stared at the muddy abstract print that hung on the wall opposite him.

"I don't know. But he was younger then. Having kids was probably a big deal for him then. By the time I came along . . . he'd been through it already."

"How about your mother?"

"She was always real big on saying how much she loved me, and all this bullshit."

"You didn't believe her?"

"Why should I? I don't think she believed it either. That's why she had to keep repeating it all the time."

Paul nodded his head.

"You know, sometimes she'd hug me and hold me. And other times, she wouldn't even let me come near her. I don't know, I think that was when she was going through the change of life. I was about seven or eight, and I remember one time going into her room. She started screaming—I mean really screaming—that I was coming after her."

"How did that make you feel?"

"Scared shitless. Here was this lady I thought was my fucking mother, and she was like this completely different person."

"Do you always talk that way?" Paul interjected.

"What way?"

"Your language. All the four-letter words."

Wally shrugged his shoulders.

"How the fuck should . . . " He stopped, then smiled.

Paul smiled back. "When did all that start?"

"Man, I don't know. Junior high school maybe."

"How come?"

"Everybody talked like that in junior high school in Jersey."

"How about your brothers? Do they still talk like that?"

"They're not saints, if that's what you mean. What are you trying to get at anyway?"

"Oh, I don't know," Paul answered equivocally. "What about women?"

"What do you mean, women?"

"Got a girlfriend?"

"No, not now. Broads and booze don't mix. I learned that a while back. I was going with this chick before I signed up for the Corps. We got it on pretty good. Anyway, when I came back, we still got it on pretty good. But when I started hitting the sauce, she didn't approve. Said her old man was a lush, and she didn't need another one in the family."

"Were you engaged?"

"No, but I guess we'd of got married if she hadn't split."

"Did that upset you, her leaving?"

"Sure it did. Except I was drinking so heavy by then, I could forget it pretty easy. Just have another drink." Wally held out his bandaged hand in front of him. It was shaking. "Shit, Doc," he said. "I could sure use one now. I don't suppose you got . . . you know, anything. I mean, I'm not fussy."

"Sorry, Wally, but that's the reason you're here. Let's get back to your girlfriend. Where were you living when she left? Were you living together?"

"No, I was in the rooming house by then."

"Rooming house?"

"Where I am now. In Passaic. I moved out of the house a couple of months after I got back."

"What made you leave your folks?"

"They were driving me nuts."

"How come?"

"Christ, Doc, I don't know. For one thing, my brother fixed me up with this hotshot job selling life insurance. He's got this agency in Red Bank. Son of a bitch has made a lot of dough. Anyway, I tried it. Do you know what it's like trying to con some poor sucker into shelling out good bucks his whole life for some bullshit policy that's gonna be worth nothing when he finally knocks off? You'd be better off putting your money in a bank."

"What happened with the job?"

"I didn't sell shit. And Mike got all bent out of shape because he felt I wasn't trying. Like he'd given me this big chance, and I wasn't appreciating it enough. Finally, I spent more time in bars than making calls, and he fired me."

"What did you do after that?"

"That's when I moved out and got this job tending bar at one of the joints where I was hanging out. Place off Route 22. It was just gonna be temporary . . . you know, till I got my act together. The rooming house was gonna be temporary, too. But then, like I said, I kept hitting the booze harder and harder, and I never went anywhere else. I'm still living in the same hole."

"Must be lonely," Paul said gently.

"Yeah, it is. I got Champ though."

"Champ?"

"My mutt. Landlady's always bitching about him. Christ, nobody lets anyone do nothing without making some big deal out of it. You ever noticed that, Doc?"

"You told me you saw a psychiatrist in the Marines, Wally. But you never told me why. Or why you were discharged. Do you want to talk a little about that now?"

"I told you. They said I was unsuitable for military service."

"Meaning?"

"I don't know. I guess I sort of flipped out toward the end."

"What happened?"

Wally looked confused and rubbed his forehead with his good hand. "You know, this is weird, but I don't really know. I can remember being out on this one operation in Beirut. And then I remember being in the hospital. But shit . . . I don't know what happened in between."

"What was the operation?"

"You remember when those assholes blew up our barracks? When they crashed a car full of explosives right into us and wasted a couple hundred guys?"

Paul nodded.

"Well, I was out on patrol when we found out about it. Anyway, we were coming back through this refugee camp . . . "

"And?"

"I don't remember. It's really nuts, but after that, my mind's a blank. Next thing I'm in a hospital. What's it mean, Doc?"

Wally looked at Paul with the eager eyes of a child. Paul responded in a fatherly voice.

"Obviously something must have happened that day that affected you a great deal. And for some reason, your conscious mind has chosen to block out the experience."

"So, it's like I'm never gonna remember it, is that it?"

"Not necessarily."

"But how can I?"

"You'd be surprised, Wally. After a few sessions, things come back to you."

Wally looked skeptical, but at the same time, he was excited by what Paul had just said. Indeed, the last forty minutes had been among the most exciting Wally had ever experienced. For the first time in his life, someone was listening to what he had to say and to what he was feeling. Even more important, Wally sensed that Paul cared about him. It was a nice feeling, a new feeling, one that he didn't quite trust yet.

"Well," Paul said, seeing by the clock on his desk that it was 6:49, "we have to stop now. But we'll talk more about Beirut next session. How do you feel?"

"All right, I guess. I didn't know I had so much to say."

"I have a hunch you have a lot more to say, Wally," Paul replied, rising and walking to his desk.

Seeing Paul get up, Wally also stood. "Uh, Doc?"

"Yes?"

"Do I pay now?"

"You can if you like, or I can bill you at the end of the month."

"Maybe you'd better do that, seeing how my brother Mike's springing for this. As a matter of fact, just send the bill direct to him. That way he won't think I'm using his money for anything else."

"Any way you like," Paul said, as Wally wrote his brother's name and address on a piece of paper.

Paul clipped the paper to the appointment book on his desk. "So," he said, escorting Wally into the hallway, "I'll see you in two days."

"Right, Doc."

Wally walked to the front door, but before opening it, he stopped and turned around. "Thanks, Doc," he said softly.

"Thanks? For what?"

"For listening. I mean, you really were listening. I could tell. It wasn't bullshit."

"Wally, that's the point."

Wally grinned. "You know, Doc, I don't even feel like I need a drink right now."

"That's good, Wally," Paul said, giving his patient a thumbs-up sign. "We're getting somewhere."

It had been a long Monday, and Paul still felt exhausted as he finished dinner at an Italian restaurant around the corner from his house. The day had started with a 9:00 A.M. staff meeting. After that, he had conducted a seminar with the residents on emergency room procedures, and then had spent the afternoon reviewing all the psychiatric cases that had been admitted over the weekend, to make sure their dispositions had been correct. Finally, there had been a supervisory hour with one of the residents, and four private patients—counting Wally—in the office at his home.

The waiter came over to Paul's table with a second cup of espresso. Sitting there with his coffee, Paul thought about the past weekend. He had planned to use it to relax, but after seeing patients on Saturday morning, he had discovered that the toilet in the third-floor bathroom was stopped up, and he had wound up spending all of Saturday trying to fix it himself. On Sunday morning, he had awakened to find water dripping down into his bedroom. The toilet had flooded the bathroom during the night, which meant that much of Sunday had been devoted to finding plumbers.

The only pleasant interlude had been playing tennis late in the day with a neighbor. But when the match was over and Paul returned home to an empty house, the reality of Vivian's being gone finally crashed down upon him with its full weight and sent him into an immobilizing depression. Whereas earlier in the day, Paul had considered going out to a movie, all he had managed to do was turn on the television set and go through a pint of ice cream. Sitting in front of the TV and stuffing himself had reminded him of the lonely, overweight child he'd been thirty years earlier, and had only compounded his depression.

Paul finished his espresso and paid the check. It was now 8:30, and the prospect of another night in front of the television set loomed before him. He thought about going home to bed, but rejected the idea. He'd learned to be very wary of exhaustion. Often, if he went to bed too early, he'd wake up at one or two in the morning, and it would take him hours to get back to sleep.

When the waiter returned with his change, Paul got up and drifted out into the Village. The street was crowded with young people and tourists. Seeing all the people made Paul feel even more lonely.

"Hey, mister. How about a quarter for something to eat?" a harsh, crackling voice asked from behind him.

Paul turned around to find an old man, painfully thin, tugging at the sleeve of his safari jacket. The man was wearing a shredded undershirt and grimy, baggy pants, but there was something about him that set him apart from the hordes of drunks and homeless that now inhabited the neighborhood. Without knowing why, Paul dug into his pocket and pulled out some change, even though he usually didn't make a practice of encouraging panhandlers. He gave the money to the old man without even bothering to see how much it was.

"God bless you, mister," the old man said, as he stumbled toward a liquor store several doors down and left Paul standing at the corner of Bleecker and Mac-

Dougal, wondering just what had inspired his charity. Then it came to him. The old man had reminded him of Max. Not Max as Paul had known him in life, but Max as he was now, hovering in the ugly netherworld between life and death.

Suddenly, Paul knew what he would do. He hadn't seen Max since last week. If he got into a cab immediately, he could be at the hospital before visiting hours were over.

Spotting a taxi a block away, Paul stepped into the street and flagged it down.

"I see you're working late tonight, Dr. Manning," said Nora Hobson, the spry little gray-haired nurse in charge of the sixth floor of New York General.

"Just thought I'd drop by and look in on Dr. Abrams," Paul replied.

"His daughter left a few minutes ago. I'm sure he'll be glad to see you, Doctor."

"Any change?" Paul asked, knowing that all changes in Max's condition from this point on would be for the worse.

"About the same."

Paul nodded and made his way down the hall to Max's room. Visiting hours were coming to a close. Families and friends were hanging about doorways, saying their good-byes. Patients in bathrobes were walking up and down the floor while they still could. Luckily, the private room Max had was off in its own little alcove, so its occupant—usually a VIP—was spared the commotion of the hallway. When Paul entered the room and again saw the spectre of his dying friend, motionless and completely covered with a sheet except for his head, he knew that Max was long past worrying about anything so trivial as a little noise outside his door.

Max's ravaged body took up so little space under the sheet that Paul was reminded of a horror film he'd seen as a kid, a film about a living head without a body. A shudder of fear went through him. Fear and revulsion. Then came guilt for feeling such ugly emotions about someone he respected and loved.

Paul walked slowly over to the bed and noticed that Max's eyes were closed. Figuring that his colleague was asleep, Paul started to leave, but was stopped by a frail voice he hardly recognized.

"Where are you going, Doctor?"

"I thought you were asleep," Paul said, returning to the bed.

"I don't sleep anymore. Sometimes the dope works a little better than others, that's all."

Paul nodded uncomfortably.

"Where have you been?" Max continued feebly. "I haven't seen you for a couple of days."

"It was one of those famous New York General Mondays," Paul explained. "And I knew your daughter was coming in this weekend. Nora Hobson told me she just left."

Max didn't answer.

"How long will Jessica be staying?" Paul asked, and instantly felt embarrassed. He knew that Jessica Abrams had come in from her home in Colorado to be with her father until the end.

"It's all right, Doctor," Max said gently. Then, all of a sudden, his face tightened in pain.

"What is it?" Paul asked, but Max's pain was so great that he didn't hear his friend.

"Oh, God! God help me!"

"Do you want a shot?"

"I just had one," Max answered, breathing heavily. After a few seconds, he seemed to relax. "It's okay, now. It's okay. It just comes . . . and goes. And there's nothing anyone can do about it."

Paul was silent.

"Do you know what the worst part is?" Max went on. "It's not the pain, the physical pain. The worst part is putting all of you people through this."

"Don't worry about us."

"You can say that, but I do worry. Jessica's got a good job in Denver, and she's left it to come here. She tells me it's just a leave of absence, but she shouldn't even have to do that. Besides, what can she do here anyway? Just sit in that chair over there and call a nurse every so often to give me more morphine. You, too, Paul. You got better things to do with your evenings than to come visit an old man."

"We wouldn't be here if we didn't want to be."

Max wasn't listening. "Feeling pain is bad enough. But what's worse is seeing it. You can see pain. I bet you didn't know that, Doctor. I can see it on your face, on Jessica's face, everywhere I look. That's when it hurts the most."

Before Paul could comment, Miss Hobson glided into the room. "Ready for bed, Doctor?" she asked Max in a cheery voice.

"I'd like to know where the hell she thinks I am," Max said to Paul as the nurse checked the I.V. and changed the water in an untouched pitcher that sat on the bedside table.

"I'll drop by tomorrow," Paul said, gently putting his hand on Max's bony shoulder.

"Thanks, Doctor Manning . . . but if you don't, that's all right, too."

"I'd like to see Jessica. It's been over a year."

"Yeah, she asked how you were."

Miss Hobson came toward Paul with a bedpan in her hand.

"I'm afraid we'll have to ask you to leave now, Doctor," she said, indicating the bedpan with a professional smile.

Paul said goodnight and left the room. It was after nine and the hallway was deserted now, except for an occasional nurse or orderly. Entering the elevator, Paul realized that his mood had changed. He no longer felt depressed. He felt angry.

He stepped out of the elevator on the lobby floor, and walked slowly toward the main entrance of the hospital. He felt dizzy, and thought about sitting down—but the moment passed quickly and left him strangely light-headed. He didn't understand it, but he knew that something was happening inside his brain. There were no clear thoughts there, only a series of disjointed images swimming around in his mind, images that he couldn't control. As he walked, he kept hearing Max's voice, saying, "There's nothing anyone can do about it." Then Paul was in bed with his wife. "Paul, what is it?" she was asking. "Please let me help, we can try again." And his own voice kept repeating, "I'm sorry, it's no use."

Over and over the same words echoed in his consciousness, until he was barely aware that, instead of leaving the hospital, he was now heading down the corridor that led to the Emergency Room. Perhaps there were some things you couldn't do anything about, the voices inside him were saying now. Things like cancer . . . like not being able to sleep . . . like not being able to make love to your wife . . . like being four years old and having a father who got drunk and liked to push you around. Perhaps there were things in life over which you had no control. But there were other things, too, things you could take care of. All you needed to do was to take charge . . . take action. Perhaps some things weren't so difficult after all.

"Still at it, Dr. Manning?" Marge Kaplan asked as Paul entered the ER.

"Still at it," Paul answered automatically. "I need the keys to the drug cabinet. Having some trouble with a private patient."

"Sure," Marge said, handing over the keys.

As Paul made his way to the cabinet, the voices seemed to be getting louder and louder. Making sure that no one was observing him, Paul slipped one of the keys into the lock and opened the metal door. From the cabinet's top shelf, he took a small vial of succinylcholine and a disposable plastic syringe, and pocketed both.

"Thanks, Marge," Paul called out, dropping the keys on her desk and heading toward the corridor, but the nurse had become so involved with a patient that she didn't even see Paul leave the room.

Nora Hobson tiptoed out of Max Abrams's room, leaving the door only slightly ajar. Every night, she looked forward to the quiet of 9:30, when all the hospital visitors had gone and the patients were in bed for the night. Now, as she made her way down the hallway, all she could think about was getting to the nurses' station and plunging into a chair.

Peace at last, she thought, seating herself and opening up a copy of the *National Enquirer* that she had been looking forward to reading all day. She was barely into a story about Elizabeth Taylor's latest diet when she became aware of a young woman standing a few yards away.

"Excuse me, are you Miss Hobson?" the woman inquired tentatively.

"Yes," Hobson answered brusquely, her tone now quite different from what it had been a few minutes ago in the presence of Dr. Manning and Dr. Abrams.

The young woman came closer to the desk. "I was told that I should talk to you," she said.

"Really?"

"I was here this afternoon . . . to see Dr. Abrams. I'm Joanna Harrison."

"So what can I do for you?" Hobson asked impatiently.

"I think I may have left something in his room. You see, I'm an actress—I mean, I'm studying to be an actress—and the script I'm working on in my class . . . well, I think it may be in Dr. Abrams's room."

"I just came from Dr. Abrams's room, and I didn't see anything like that in there."

"It's not very big. I remember putting it on the radiator with my purse. I think it may have slipped off."

"Visiting hours are over, Miss . . . what did you say your name was?"

"Harrison."

"Miss Harrison. I'm afraid I really can't help you. All I can tell you is to check back tomorrow."

"But I have to do my scene in class tomorrow

morning, and I had counted on going over the script again tonight."

"I'm sorry, Miss Harrison, you'll have to come back tomorrow."

"I could go look for it myself."

"I said visiting hours are over," the nurse answered adamantly.

"Oh, please," Joanna begged, almost crying. "I'll make such a fool of myself, if I don't know my lines."

Hobson drummed her fingers on her desk. "You know where his room is?"

"Yes, I've been there quite often these last few weeks."

"You know, of course, that it's highly irregular. However, if you promise to go right in and out, I'll let you do it this one time. I'd do it myself, except this is the first time I've been off my feet in three hours. Now, he may be asleep, so be sure not to wake him."

Joanna thanked Miss Hobson and started toward Max's room. Within seconds, however, she realized that she had only known the sixth floor by day, during afternoon visiting hours, or during evening visiting hours, when it was brightly lit. Tonight, there was something distinctly eerie and foreboding about the place, and she suddenly wished that the cranky nurse had come with her.

When she reached the end of the main hallway, she stopped and tried to collect her thoughts before turning the corner to the small alcove that led to Dr. Abrams's room. If he were still awake, she didn't want to frighten him. At the same time, the idea of going into the room, with him lying there asleep, scared her. Either way, it was going to be unpleasant. Finally, she drew up as much courage as she could and forced herself to turn the corner.

Her mind now made up, she walked quickly toward the room. She knew it was silly for her to feel afraid, but then she had felt afraid so often lately. Almost constantly. That was why she had been seeing Dr. Abrams in the first place.

Passing the stairwell, she automatically looked through its windowed doors . . . just in case someone was lurking there. To her surprise, she saw the back of a blond man in a safari jacket going down the stairs. But, far from being frightened by him, Joanna felt almost comforted. She realized that she had seen the man before—he was the doctor she had met in front of Dr. Abrams's room, several days earlier. Probably on his way home now, or perhaps he'd been called in to handle an emergency. She was sorry to see him disappear down the stairs, because now she was again faced with the prospect of going into Dr. Abrams's room alone.

She hesitated a moment, then pushed open the door and stepped into the room. Looking at the bed, she saw that Dr. Abrams was in a deep sleep. All she heard as she went to the radiator was the hum of the air-conditioning system, which masked the noise of the street outside. Carefully, she got down on her knees and felt around the floor for the script. Just as she had guessed, it was below the radiator, and she retrieved it easily.

Standing up, she glanced over at the bed again. Dr. Abrams was completely motionless. Indeed, Joanna was amazed by how quiet everything seemed. She could still hear the air-conditioner and the muffled street noises, but the quiet she sensed seemed to emanate from the room itself . . . a quiet far more intense than these background sounds. Suddenly, Joanna felt afraid again, and standing there, she understood why.

It was obvious. Dr. Abrams wasn't breathing. He wasn't moving. The silence in the room was death.

Her fear turning to panic, Joanna rushed out of the room and down the hallway to the nurses' station.

"Miss Hobson! Miss Hobson!" she cried out. "Dr. Abrams . . . come quickly! It's Dr. Abrams!"

"What are you talking about?" Hobson asked, angrily putting down her tabloid.

"I think he's dead!"

Without saying a word, Miss Hobson got up and raced down the hall, Joanna following closely behind.

The moment she reached the bedside, Nora Hobson knew that the young woman had not been mistaken. She felt for Max's pulse, certain that she would find nothing. She had worked around death too long, and she knew exactly what it looked like, felt like, smelled like. Joanna watched as the nurse then lifted Max's eyelids open for further confirmation of his death.

"Well, it's a blessing, that's all I can say," Hobson's sober voice announced as she closed the lids. "He's out of pain at last. He deserves to be."

"Yes . . . a blessing," Joanna agreed, but as she looked at Dr. Abrams's lifeless form, tears began streaming down her face. He had been so kind to her, so good to her, right up to the end. Now that he was gone, she didn't know what she was going to do.

July 11

They buried Max this morning in Queens. Beautiful day. More like fall than July. Air crisp—incredible view of Manhattan. Couldn't tell where the cemetery stopped and the skyline began. Gravestones like miniature skyscrapers—and the real skyscrapers like gravestones. Beautiful.

Service at Temple short and simple. No flowers, no hymns, no incense. So different from when Pop drank himself to death. I still remember that long, depressing requiem mass. But today, just a few prayers. Don't know when I last felt so peaceful and relaxed. And when they lowered the casket into the ground, all I could think about was the look on Max's face just before he died. When he thanked me with his eyes.

Now I must continue his work. At the end of service, an omen! Girl with pretty blue eyes from outside Max's room last week comes up to the car. She was crying and seemed fairly strung out. Said how much Max meant to her as a therapist. Asked if she could see me professionally. At first, I told her I couldn't. But she kept on crying, practically begging me. Touching. Very touching. Finally, I told her to call me for an appointment. After all, that's what Max would have wanted, isn't it? And I guess I sort of owe him something.

II.

July 17

"Wally," Paul asked, leaning forward in his chair, "have you ever been hypnotized?"

The question caught Wally Darrow off guard. He was midway into his fourth session with Paul, struggling again to remember just what had happened in Lebanon that resulted in his discharge.

"You mean like you see on television?"

"Well, that's one kind of hypnotism. But it also happens to be a very useful technique in therapy. It can save a lot of time. And since time is money, it can save a lot of that, too."

"That'll make my brother happy," Wally said cynically. "But I don't know, Doc. Hypnotism? It sounds sort of weird."

"Are you afraid?"

"Kind of . . . I guess."

"There's nothing to be afraid of. I'd only use it with your consent."

"But Christ, Doc, how do I know what I'll do when I'm under?"

"There's nothing to worry about. You won't do anything you wouldn't ordinarily do. And you can't be made to do anything you don't want to do. It's just that, in cases like yours, hypnosis can help us get to a lot of things much faster."

"Like Beirut?" Wally asked, swallowing hard.

"Exactly. Of course, there's always the possibility that you may not be receptive. No one can be hypnotized if he doesn't want to be. And some people who are willing still aren't good subjects."

"How can you tell if I'd go under?"

"We can only try it, and see what happens."

Wally opened and closed his sweating hands as he weighed the proposition. He both feared the idea, and found it intriguing. In just a few sessions, he had become quite taken with the whole experience of therapy, and had come to see it as an adventure, a journey to some unknown country in which he was the explorer and Paul was his trusted guide. So far, the traveling had been smooth, he thought, so why stop now? After all, the country he was exploring was his life, and he had lived twenty-seven years knowing very little about it.

He looked at Paul and shrugged his shoulders. "Shit, Doc. I guess I don't have all that much to lose."

"And a lot to gain," Paul added, as he rose from his chair and started closing the drapes of the two windows that faced MacDougal Street.

"Do you always do that?" Wally asked apprehensively.

"The point is for you to try to be as relaxed as possible," Paul answered reassuringly. He walked to the light switches and dimmed the overhead track lights, carefully focused on the various paintings, prints, and plants that decorated the office. The only light in the room now emanated from a small white globe that sat on his desk.

"Just relax," Paul said, returning to his chair, his voice now soft and soothing. "Think of something pleasant, some place where you'd like to be. Maybe a beach, or in the mountains. A nice, pleasant, peaceful place. Just close your eyes and relax all of your muscles, and think of how peaceful everything is."

Wally closed his eyes.

"Now," Paul continued, his voice becoming slightly more forceful, "imagine that you are going into a deep, deep sleep. Your arms are getting heavy, your legs are getting heavy, your eyelids are getting very, very heavy. Your eyelids are so heavy that in a few seconds you won't be able to open them, no matter how hard you try. Your eyelids are very, very heavy."

Wally was breathing deeply and regularly. To all appearances, he was fast asleep in his chair.

"Okay, I want you to try something, Wally. Your eyelids are so heavy that you won't be able to open your eyes. But I want you to try to open them anyway. You won't be able to, but try."

Wally heard Paul and attempted to open his eyes. He managed to raise his eyebrows a little, but his eyes stayed closed.

"Now, relax," Paul said gently. "Relax your eye muscles. You are now sound asleep, and you will not awaken until I tell you. When I do, you will awaken quietly and easily. I am going to ask you a few questions, Wally. Simple questions. Even though you are asleep, you can still hear me, and you will be able to answer me. You will not wake up, but you will have no trouble at all answering my questions. First of all, Wally, tell me how old you are."

Wally spoke in a slow, colorless voice. "I am twenty-seven years old."

"And where do you live?"

"I live at 457 Main Avenue, Passaic, New Jersey."

"And your phone number?"

"I don't have a phone. Disconnected."

"You told me once that you have a dog, is that correct?"

"Right."

"Okay, Wally, listen carefully. You will not wake up until I tell you. You will not wake up, but when I count to three, you will open your eyes. You will open your eyes, but you will still be asleep. And when you open your eyes, you will see your dog. He'll be sitting on your lap. Okay. One . . . two . . . three."

Wally's eyes opened. He looked down at his lap and started petting the air in front of him.

"What are you doing, Wally?"

"It's Champ. I think he's hungry."

"There's a bowl of food behind your chair. If you put Champ on the floor, he'll go back there and eat it."

Wally pantomimed lifting something from his lap onto the floor.

"Okay, Wally," Paul continued softly. "We're going on a long, long journey. Out of New York. Out of the United States. We're going to go to the Middle East. We're going to go back a few years, too. You've been out on patrol, and you're returning to your barracks. Only you've just found out they've been bombed. A lot of men in your company have been killed."

Wally's eyes stared vacantly at the print on the far wall.

"What do you see, Wally?"

"A camp," Wally answered, as his gaze became more intense.

"Describe the camp."

"Tents. Lots of gray canvas. And dusty streets. Filled with shit and piss. It stinks."

"Are there any people, Wally?"

"Yeah. Mostly women."

"Tell me about them."

"They're all standing together. There are about ten of them. A couple of old men and some kids, too."

"What are you doing?"

"We're standing there and . . . "

"What?" Paul demanded.

"We've got our weapons aimed at the people."

"Yes? Go on."

Wally didn't reply.

"What are you going to do?"

"We're . . . "

"Go on!"

"We're going to waste one of them." Emotion flooded Wally's voice.

"Why?"

"Because she helped the fuckers who blew up our barracks."

"She?"

"Yeah. She's shaking her fist and bragging that she loaded the bombs into the car that drove into the barracks. She's spitting, too. 'I spit on America,' she's saying. Her English sucks but we can understand her. And the others are spitting and shaking their fists, too."

"And what are you doing?"

"Our lieutenant is shouting at us."

"What's he saying?"

"That we've got to teach these scumbags a lesson. He's making us all point our guns at the lead woman. It's like a firing squad. Only . . . "

"What?"

"Only . . . my gun is still down. I can't do it, and the son of a bitch is starting in on me now."

"What do you mean?"

"The lieutenant . . . he's calling me a pussy. He's saying I'm scared to kill her. He's saying I'm a candy-ass traitor because I'm afraid to kill her."

"Are you scared?"

"Yeah, I don't want to do it."

"What's happening now?"

"A couple of our guys are pulling her away from the crowd. Closer to me. They're gonna make me do it all by myself."

"And the lieutenant?"

"He's saying the woman has more guts than I do."

"Does she?"

"No! Shit, no! But now they're practically shoving her in my face and she's starting to scream. She's starting to scream like crazy—in Arabic. It's half angry and half scared. It's the loudest goddamned shrieking I've ever heard. And the lieutenant's calling me a pussy again. He's yelling at me to waste her. And the woman's wailing even louder. Christ, I can't stand it. If only she'd stop, I wouldn't have to do it to her . . . but it's so fucking loud, like it's never going to stop. Oh Christ, I . . . I can't take it. I gotta stop her from making all that noise. It's just like my fucking mother when I was a kid and went into her room . . ."

Suddenly, Wally stopped and sat perfectly still.

"What is it?" Paul asked.

"I had to do it," Wally answered simply. "I had to waste her. She wouldn't stop screaming."

"It's all right, Wally," Paul said, a note of triumph in his voice. "I know you had to. It's all right. I want you just to take it easy now. You're going to wake up soon. When you do, you're going to feel very relaxed. You'll remember about the woman, but you'll be able to face it. You won't be scared any longer. Now, I'm going to count to five. By the time I reach five, you'll be wide-awake and you'll feel fine. One . . . you're waking up. Two . . . you're still waking up. Three . . . you're almost awake. Four . . . you're just about there."

On five, Paul snapped his fingers. Wally shook his head and looked around. His eyes were now sharp and focused.

"How do you feel?" Paul asked.

"Okay," Wally replied, sounding surprised.

"You're a good subject," Paul said approvingly. "That's a good sign. It means we can make progress." Wally smiled. He liked pleasing Paul. "Do you remember anything?"

"No, nothing. Except . . . "

"Except what?"

"Jesus Christ! Beirut! That fucking camp!" he exclaimed. At the same time he looked stunned. "That woman! Oh, Christ. I blew her face away, Doc. That was it. That was what I couldn't remember."

"How do you feel now?"

"Lousy."

"Lousy . . . how?"

"Ashamed," Wally answered, rubbing his eyes in an effort to mask the tears.

"Is that all?"

Wally gave Paul a confused look and started to cry in earnest. "It's crazy, Doc. But I feel . . . I don't know how to put it exactly."

"Put it any way you like."

"I feel . . . lighter. That's it, lighter. Like I lost something that was loading me down."

Paul leaned forward. "That's just what you did,

Wally. You did lose something. It's good to let things out in the open, even painful things."

Wally continued to sob.

"That's all right," Paul said. "Just let it out. I'm here. You've got someone with you."

Wally gazed at Paul appreciatively, then took a tissue from the box on the table next to him and wiped his eyes.

"You know, Doc, I think this is the first time I cried in about ten years. Really cried, I mean."

"I know, Wally. I know." Paul got up and walked over to his desk.

"Is it time?"

"I'm afraid it is. Will you be okay? Perhaps you'd like a few minutes to pull yourself together?"

"I'll be all right, Doc," Wally answered, smiling and crying at the same time. He blew his nose, stood up, and took another tissue from the box. "One for the road!" he joked, holding up the tissue as he walked to the door.

Paul smiled back and opened the door. "See you Thursday."

"Oh Doc, about Thursday. If I'm a little late, don't worry about it. It's because I may be getting a job."

"Oh, really? Doing what?"

"I almost forgot to tell you," Wally went on enthusiastically. "I have an interview for this job at an Exxon station over in Hoboken. I'd be pumping gas again for a while, but the guy I talked to on the phone said I could be an assistant manager in three months if I work out."

"Hey, Wally, that's great. You can tell me more about it on Thursday."

"Thanks, Doc. I figured you'd want to know . . . especially since I owe it all to you."

Paul smiled and nodded uneasily as he watched Wally leave. He was flattered by the growing role Wally seemed to be assigning him in his life, but he was also afraid. The more important he became to Wally, the more responsible he felt for what happened to him.

But that was what psychotherapy was all about: people paying money for someone to talk to, someone to believe in, someone to be important in their lives. Could Paul help it if he was sometimes particularly skillful at making an impression on his patients?

Back inside his office, Paul sat at his desk, closed his eyes, and tried to relax before his next patient arrived. Joanna Harrison was scheduled to have her first session in five minutes. Five minutes, and it would all start over again—the delicate maneuver of trying to help someone, while at the same time keeping one's distance. It shouldn't have to be that way, Paul thought—but it was the only way he could survive.

Despite her shyness, Joanna Harrison spoke with considerable ease about herself. This surprised Paul and also pleased him. In a mere half hour, Joanna had provided him with enough details of her history for him to pick up where Max had left off.

Her story was all too familiar. Small-town girl from the Midwest defies her strait-laced family to come to New York to be an actress. Only to find life in the big city lonely and tough going. The stuff of 1930s B movies—right down to her room in a residential hotel in the theater district.

There was an ugly twist to her story, and it was

because of this that she had started therapy. When she got to this point in her tale, Joanna had a considerably harder time telling it.

"Go on," Paul urged gently. "You were describing the man in your acting class."

"His name was Jack. He was very tall and very thin. He had the blackest hair I'd ever seen. There was something poetic about him."

"Were you attracted to him?" Paul asked matter-of-factly.

"I . . . I guess I was. But I never said a word to him until Maria assigned us a scene together."

"What was that?"

"It was from *The Glass Menagerie*. The one between the crippled young girl, Laura, and the gentleman caller her mother has arranged to pay her a visit."

"Did it go well?"

"Well!" Joanna gave a look of disgust. "It was awful. Maria really let us have it, too. Especially Jack. She accused him of being totally unreal in the scene. Said he was performing totally for himself. She even compared his acting to masturbating on stage."

"How did he take it?"

"He didn't say a word at the time, but we had coffee after the class and he let loose. Maria was full of crap, he said. She hadn't made it in the theater, which was why she was teaching. All acting schools did was keep people from being successful. I tried to reason with him, but that only made things worse. He even accused me of trying to make him look bad in the scene. When he stormed out, I figured I'd seen the last of him."

"But you hadn't."

"He called me that evening. He was very apologetic and asked me to meet him the following night for dinner. He said that, of all the people in the class, I was the only one who was worth anything. I don't know, I guess I felt sorry for him, because I agreed to go out with him. He gave me his address. It was way over in the East Village, on Third Street and Avenue C—but when I got there, it turned out to be an abandoned tenement building."

"What did you do then?"

"I decided to leave and go back uptown, but just as I started to go, I spotted him coming down the street. He looked—I don't know exactly how to say it—different."

"How do you mean?"

"He was wearing a black leather jacket that I'd never seen him in before. He had on these high black boots, too, and black jeans. What was really strange was that he had pinned this bright red carnation to his jacket. It was creepy."

"Creepy?"

"He was all in black, except for this splash of red."

"What did you say to him when you saw him?"

"I asked him why he had given me the wrong address."

"And what did he say to that?"

"He just smiled and took my arm and said he had his own special place in the building, one that nobody else knew about. I told him to let go of me, but he only held my arm tighter and—" She stopped and looked away from Paul.

"What is it?"

"This is the hard part, Doctor."

"I'm sure it is—but don't stop now. It's important."

Staring at the floor, Joanna went on.

"He started walking me down the outside stairs that led to the basement. I don't know why, but I couldn't scream. It wasn't until he was dragging me into the basement that I was able to make any sound at all, but then it was too late."

"Why?"

"Because now he stuffed a handkerchief into my mouth. Then he shoved me down a corridor and kept calling me all of these horrible names. He kept saying that I was the reason the scene in class hadn't been good, that I had deliberately sabotaged his work.

"There was a room at the end of the passageway. He pushed me inside. He must have put candles in the room earlier. They cast this horrible glow over everything. There were posters on the walls and the ceiling—sick posters of people in leather outfits, doing all sorts of obscene things to one another. He clicked open a switchblade and said I'd have to pay for what I'd done to him. The thing that scared me most wasn't the knife though . . . "

"What was it?"

"It was his smile. It was the ugliest smile I've ever seen. When he ripped off my coat, all I was conscious of was that horrible smile and the blood red carnation. Then he yanked off my blouse, my bra, and finally my skirt. He told me not to move, that if I did, he couldn't be responsible for what might happen.

"He threw the knife down and took off his pants. He came down on top of me and forced himself inside me and—"

Again she stopped.

"I understand how painful this must be for you, but try. Remember, you're not alone."

"I guess I started to retch, but I was gagged and I started choking. I didn't care about dying anymore. I wanted to. I really did. He just kept pounding away, and all the while the red carnation was right up against my face."

Tears were now streaming down her face. Paul indicated the box of tissues on the table next to her.

"Thanks, Dr. Manning," she said, taking a tissue. She dabbed her eyes and blew her nose. "I'm sorry," she said, shaking her head.

"You're a brave young woman," Paul said softly.

"And a stupid young woman."

"Why do you say that?"

"I let him get away with it. I never went to the police. I didn't do anything."

"What about your parents?"

"I wanted to tell them, but I couldn't. I kept feeling that what happened was my fault, that I had it coming to me because I went to New York . . . because I broke the rules."

"But it wasn't your fault. You realize that, don't you?"

"In my head, yes. But my feelings were something else. After it happened, I couldn't sleep. And when I did, I kept having nightmares. Eventually, I knew I had to talk to someone, so I looked up hospitals in the phone book. I saw that New York General wasn't too far from the hotel, and after another couple of days, I pulled myself together enough to call. That's how I became Dr. Abrams's patient."

"And now mine," Paul added warmly.

"And now yours." Joanna smiled. "Thank God for both of you."

3:00 A.M. Wide-awake. Mom picks middle of night to call me to tell me she's lonely. Christ! Interrupts crazy dream. In bed with Vivian who asks why I'm wearing my leather jacket. Next, it's not my wife, it's Joanna Harrison, and I'm screwing her. She's moaning for more and I'm really getting turned on, practically coming, when —Mom!

Is her call a signal? A warning? Know I'm attracted to Joanna. Knew that this afternoon in session. She's vulnerable the way Vivian used to be when I first met her at Harvard. But she's also my patient. Forget it! Especially now that the chairmanship is within my grasp. Had lunch with Alec Graham today. I'm a little tense, but it goes well.

Is the tide turning??? Even private practice becoming more satisfying. Hypnosis with Darrow kid works magnificently. I turn him from hostile punk into grateful puppy dog. Something exciting about being able to mold someone into what they should be.

Only disturbing note: squash game today. My game very off, but it wasn't that. Something else—something very bizarre. Max. For a second, I thought I saw him out of the corner of my eye—watching me play, keeping his eye on my every move.

Hey, old man. Stay out of this, okay?

July 18

"Are you sure I can't get you another cognac?" Elena Rothman asked Paul as she filled a large snifter with Grand Marnier for herself. The last group of dinner guests had just left.

"No, thank you," Paul replied, sneaking a look at his watch and seeing that it was almost eleven. "I really should be going, too. I didn't get much sleep last night."

"And what were we up to, Paulie?" Elena inquired, her usually precise speech slightly slurred.

"Nothing really," Paul answered. "I just couldn't sleep, that's all."

"But you're a bachelor now, darling," she said playfully as she sat down opposite Paul on the L-shaped leather sofa in her living room. "You should be out living it up. What are separate vacations for, anyway?"

As she spoke, Elena toyed with a tiny wooden mask that hung round her neck and dangled in front of her cleavage. She was wearing a low-cut, high-waisted sundress that emphasized her large breasts but managed to hide the rest of her matronly body fairly successfully.

"I guess the timing is wrong," Paul responded. "I'm so up to my ears in work right now that I barely have time to get in a half hour of exercise, much less go out on the town."

Elena, realizing that her guest was having a hard time taking his eyes off the wooden mask that she continued to fondle, looked amused.

"It's from Senegal, darling," she said. "Do you approve?"

[81]

"It's . . . very unusual," Paul answered, blushing slightly.

"It's a fertility god," she said. Then she gave a loud laugh. "A hell of a lot of good it did me tonight!"

"What do you mean?"

"You didn't notice?"

"Notice what?"

"My friend Bill."

"You mean the guy who came here for drinks before dinner?"

"He was supposed to stay a lot longer than drinks, darling."

"Sorry." Paul hadn't realized that the tall, slightly pudgy stockbroker was Elena's boyfriend from Weight Watchers.

"I guess it serves me right—for playing around with children. What do you think, Doctor? A woman pushing fifty, two divorces, no kids, afraid of getting old? I'm sure there's some Freudian explanation for the whole thing, isn't there? What's the answer?"

"After fifteen years in this business, Elena, the one thing I've learned is that there are no simple answers to anything."

"God, it must be depressing to be a shrink. It's depressing enough just having one's own problems, but to be saddled with everybody else's, too. I don't know how you do it, Paulie. I certainly don't envy you."

"I don't either," he said, putting his empty glass on the coffee table. "Especially when I think of the day I have ahead of me tomorrow."

"All the more reason to stay just where you are and relax a few more minutes. Another drink never hurt anyone." Before he could refuse, Elena scooped up Paul's glass and took it to the bar. "I absolutely won't allow you to leave without a nightcap."

"I really should be getting home," Paul protested.

"But darling, you practically are home!" Elena countered, presenting Paul with a large shot of cognac.

"You know," she said, sitting down next to him on the sofa, "I went to a psychiatrist once. It was after my last divorce, right before you and Vivian moved to the garden. I think I saw the man for about six weeks. He was so calm—that's what got me about him. He was so incredibly relaxed. I'd go to see him and I'd be foaming at the mouth, and here he was, the absolute picture of tranquility. I thought, God, if only I could be like him, everything would be all right."

"And was it?"

"Ha! Do you know what happened? The bastard went and killed himself on me! I mean, if it hadn't been so tragic, it would have been hilarious. Of all the thousands of shrinks in this city, I wind up with one that puts a bullet through his head six weeks after I start therapy. It was in the papers. Maybe you remember it?"

"Vaguely," Paul answered. "You know, Elena, psychiatrists have problems, too."

"Oh, I'm sure some do. I bet you don't, Paulie."

"That's where you're wrong."

"But look at you, darling. You and Vivian. The two of you are so . . . perfect. I mean, here you are—you have a lovely home, two beautiful children. You're successful. And on top of that, for a man your age, you have one of the best bodies I've ever seen."

Paul smiled awkwardly. "I think you're exaggerating just a bit there, Elena."

"Do you think I'm making a pass at you?" she asked lightly.

"I . . . I don't know," Paul answered honestly.

"Well, I am." Her voice was very serious now.

"I see," Paul said simply.

A long silence followed. Elena, her eyes somewhat glazed from the wine she had served at dinner plus the two Grand Marniers she had just consumed, kept staring at Paul.

He knew it was crazy, but suddenly he found himself obsessed with the idea of going to bed with Elena Rothman. At the same time, he was amused. Could it be that he would end his two-month period of impotence with his next-door neighbor? He looked at the little carved mask that hung round Elena's neck. It seemed to be smiling at Paul—inviting him to go ahead and make love to her. In a strange way, he felt that there was something magic about the little figure, as if this totem had the power to make him a man again.

Almost involuntarily, Paul's hands found their way to Elena's breasts, his thumbs easily separating the loose fabric of the bodice of her dress to expose them. The little god continued to smile as Paul started kissing her nipples.

"Oh, Dr. Manning," Elena cried, moaning in pleasure. "We've had this appointment for a long time."

He slid his hand up her leg and reached under her skirt.

"Oh yes, Paulie," she said, sighing in ecstasy, "but let's go upstairs. We don't want the neighbors to see!"

Paul withdrew his hand from between Elena's legs. Then he looked once more at the pendant round her neck. Slowly and dramatically, he took it in his fingers and kissed it.

Elena laughed. "Well, it looks like my little friend isn't letting me down after all," she said, rising and leading Paul to the staircase.

Red was the predominant color of Elena's bedroom: red wallpaper, red slat blinds, red satin spread on a large brass bed.

"You've never seen my little boudoir, have you, darling?" Elena cooed. "Bathroom's to the left," she instructed as she slipped out of her dress and adjusted the blinds. At the same time, Paul removed his shirt.

"Divine chest, Dr. Manning," Elena said, sizing up Paul from across the room. "I was right about that physique of yours. Best in the garden."

She slinked toward him. With one hand she examined his well-developed pectoral muscles, while the other made its way to his crotch.

"We've got to get you out of these trousers, Doctor," she went on, undoing his belt, unzipping his fly, and peeling off his jeans and undershorts. Paul stepped out of his loafers and the heap of clothes that had accumulated at his feet.

"And now, let's go to bed," Elena said, with a dramatic flick of her hand. "And Paulie, darling," she added, looking down at his feet, "do me a favor and take off your socks. I have this thing about fucking a man with his socks on. Turns me off."

Paul removed his socks as asked, noticing as he bent down that he was losing his erection.

"Come on, Doctor. Show me your stuff."

Trying to ignore the anxiety that was beginning to take hold of him, Paul walked slowly over to the bed.

"Look up, baby. Look at the ceiling," Elena commanded. "Isn't it divine?"

Paul looked up and saw that Elena had installed mirrored squares above her bed.

"I like to know what's happening—from every angle!" she purred, pulling Paul down on top of her.

Paul had a hunch that it was already too late. As Elena held up her breasts for Paul to fondle, he caught a glimpse of her African pendant once again. Only now the thing no longer seemed to be smiling.

"What is it, Paulie?" Elena asked as he backed away from her.

"No!" Paul screamed, turning on his side.

"What in God's name is wrong?"

Paul was certain that he had just seen Max's face.

"Jesus Christ!" Elena snapped, totally baffled by the man who now lay beside her in a tense fetal position. "What is the matter with you?"

"Nothing," Paul answered weakly, realizing at the same time that he must get hold of himself. "My stomach, that's all. I think I might be getting an ulcer."

"An ulcer!" Elena shrieked. "An ulcer *now*? This minute? What the hell are you talking about?"

"I don't know. I had some kind of attack just then, that's all."

"Well, are you going to fuck me or what?"

"I . . . I don't know."

"You don't know!" Elena laughed angrily. "Now I've heard everything! The good doctor doesn't know! So just when do you expect to let me in on your plans?"

"Look," Paul said, feeling he had to get out of the red hell of Elena's bedroom immediately, "I think maybe I'm going to throw up."

"Well, don't do it on the carpet, darling," Elena replied with disgust.

"I'm sorry. I think maybe I'd better leave. Maybe some other time."

"Forget it, Doctor. Life is too short."

"Sorry," Paul repeated, getting back into his pants. Elena eyed him coldly from her bed.

"Don't be sorry on my account, darling. I think the only person any of us has to feel sorry for is Vivian. No wonder she's off in the Mediterranean. It's all so—how shall I say—more dependable over there."

Paul felt as if his face were on fire. If he had been closer to Elena, he would have belted her, but he was standing in the doorway, and she was across the room. He picked up his shirt and pulled it over his head.

"Bye, bye, Paulie!" she taunted from her red bed. "I think I'd prescribe Vitamin E, but then, I'm not the doctor. You are!"

Paul clenched his fists, then turned around, and headed for the staircase. Coming up the stairs, he had wanted to make love to Elena Rothman. Now, all he could think about was murdering the bitch.

July 19

It was already a two-Valium day for Paul. There had been a staff meeting, a session with the residents on malpractice suits, a couple of private consultations, a lousy lunch of lukewarm chili in the cafeteria, and, last but not least, a phone call from Alec Graham asking Paul to write a detailed proposal on how he would restructure the psychiatry department of New York General if he were chairman. Far from being flattered, Paul was furious at having to audition for a job that he considered to be rightfully his. If he had been an outsider, perhaps a proposal would be called for, but he had been on the staff at the hospital far too long to be treated in this shabby way.

Paul stared at the legal pad on the desk in his office at the hospital. He had jotted down a few notes for Graham's proposal, but as his anger had intensified he had crossed all of them out. His eyes now moved to his Rolodex, which displayed the name and phone number of a Dr. Morton, a fellow psychiatrist. Five years ago, Paul had been Morton's patient. At the time, Paul was in the throes of buying the townhouse on MacDougal Street, and had taken on an extremely heavy load of private patients to help with the expenses. He had been totally exhausted. Morton had helped him put his professional and personal lives into perspective. Now, Paul wondered if he should call the doctor again.

But instead of dialing the phone or working on the proposal for Graham, Paul just sat at his desk without moving. So deep was his present state of inertia that he barely heard the phone ringing. On the fifth ring, however, he snapped out of it and picked up the receiver. Nora Hobson, the sixth-floor head nurse, was on the other end of the line.

"Oh, Dr. Manning, I'm sorry to disturb you," she said. "But Dr. D'Amico has requested a psychiatric consult for one of our patients up here, and I noticed that you're still in the building."

"What's the problem?"

"AIDS patient, possibly suicidal."

"Okay, Nora. I'll be up as soon as I can."

"Thanks, Doctor."

Paul hung up the phone and glanced again at the Rolodex and the scribblings on the legal pad.

"Later," he said to himself as he tore the top sheet from the pad, crumpled it, and threw it into the wastebasket. He reached into his pocket, took out his gold box of Valium, and opened it for the third time that day. He had no water, so he simply put a tablet onto his tongue and swallowed it. He gulped a few times to make sure it had reached his stomach, then got up, put on his jacket, and took off for Hobson's floor.

In the elevator, Paul was filled with a sense of foreboding. This was the first time he had been on the floor since Max Abrams's death. Walking down the corridor to the nurses' station, Paul deliberately kept his eyes focused on the floor to avoid catching sight of the alcove where his late colleague's room had been.

"I'm really sorry to disturb you, Doctor," Nora Hobson said. "I realize that you've probably had a long day."

"Where is the patient?"

"Six-eighteen. Here's his chart. Dr. D'Amico's observations are inside."

"Thanks, Nora." Paul took the folder from the nurse and scanned the attending physician's notes. The patient was a thirty-four-year-old man who had been hospitalized with pneumocystis pneumonia, an opportunistic infection common in AIDS patients. It was the young man's third hospitalization. Earlier in the day, he had made a halfhearted attempt to slash his wrists with a shattered plastic glass.

"Is he quiet now?" Paul asked without looking up from the chart.

"He may even be asleep."

"Pretty hard to kill yourself with a piece of plastic," Paul observed wryly.

Hobson raised her eyebrow and started talking in a confidential tone of voice.

"It turns out he had a fight with his lover this morning," she said, taking a devilish delight in her little piece of sixth-floor gossip. "That's what brought on the incident. Then, the two of them made up, had a good cry, and that was that. I don't know why Dr. D'Amico requested the consult in the first place."

"We both know that Dr. D'Amico does everything strictly by the book," Paul observed, putting down the chart.

"Speaking of that," Hobson added, without going out of her confidential mode, "I've been meaning to ask you about something, Dr. Manning."

"What's that?"

"It's about Dr. Abrams."

"Max?" Paul tried to appear calm, but the dread he had felt when he came onto the floor was back again in full force.

"I just wanted to know if it was you who ordered the autopsy?"

Paul clenched his fist around the pillbox in his pocket.

"Autopsy? What are you talking about?"

"You mean, you didn't know about it?"

"No, I didn't."

"Oh, I'm so relieved."

"Relieved? I'm afraid you've really lost me, Nora."

"Well, you see, it's just that he died on my floor when I was on duty. And when I heard about the autopsy, I thought that maybe you might have ordered it to check up on something we might have done up here. I know how close you two were. I guess I was being a little paranoid, that's all, Doctor."

"He was a dying man," Paul pointed out, sounding more defensive than he intended. "Everyone at this hospital did all that was humanly possible to make him comfortable right up to the end. There was nothing unusual about his death."

"So why do you think there was an autopsy?"

"I don't know. Perhaps his family requested it. Perhaps it was in his will. This is a teaching hospital, after all. Whatever it was, there's nothing for you to be concerned about, Nora."

"Oh, thank you, Dr. Manning," the nurse responded with genuine gratitude. "I've been here for thirty-six years and there's no one prouder of their work than I am. I just hated the thought that somebody might question it."

"As I said, Nora, you have nothing to worry about."

Paul gave a professional smile and headed off to

the patient in 618, this time even more careful to avoid looking up. When he reached the room, he couldn't help but see the corridor that led to what had been Max's deathbed. An eerie, amber glow emanated from the space. A trick of the afternoon light, Paul told himself. Still, his head started to pound and his hands turned cold.

"Goddammit, old man," Paul said to himself, unable to erase the image of Max's face that now popped up in his mind. "I thought I told you to stay out of this."

"So this asshole manager tells me I can't go home until I clean out the rest rooms."

Wally Darrow was explaining why he had quit his job after just one day, but Paul found it hard to listen. The vision of Max still haunted him, and he couldn't stop thinking about what Hobson had revealed to him earlier that afternoon. Of course, Paul tried to assure himself for yet another time, the whole autopsy business probably meant nothing. A routine pathology examination wouldn't turn up anything unusual in Max's case. Still, he couldn't be one hundred percent sure.

"Can you imagine that, Doc?" Wally went on, oblivious to his therapist's problems. "This is the hot-shit job that's gonna have me an assistant manager in three months, and they want me to scrub toilets." Paul didn't respond and Wally seemed hurt. "So?"

"So? So what?" Paul said indifferently.

"I mean that guy was really an asshole, wasn't he?"

"I don't know, Wally," Paul answered. His Valium

was wearing off and his patience was wearing thin. "When you take a job, you have to start somewhere."

"Somewhere, sure. But not shoveling shit."

"Perhaps not. But it sounds as though you didn't give it much of a chance."

"Wait a minute, Doc," Wally said angrily. "Who's side are you on, anyway?"

"It's not about sides, Wally." There was anger in Paul's voice now as well.

"Then what *is* it about, goddammit? I trusted you, man. And now you're starting to shit all over me, too."

"Now you wait a minute," Paul blurted out, no longer concerned about hiding his disgust with Wally's behavior. "What kind of baby talk is that?"

"Baby talk?" Wally was stunned.

"Yes. You sound like a big overgrown baby, and at your age, it's pretty pathetic."

Wally exploded. "You bastard," he yelled. "You're just like everybody else! My fucking mother. My fucking father! My fucking brothers!"

"Stop whining, Wally!" Paul shouted back. "Stop acting like the world owes you a living. You're not a kid anymore. You're a man. It's about time you started acting like one."

Wally stood up and shook his fist at Paul. "Son of a bitch! You betrayed me!"

"Nobody betrayed you," Paul snapped back, rising and taking a step toward Wally, who was now at the door. "And where do you think you're going?"

"I'm outta here, man."

"No, Wally," Paul said, moving toward the door and realizing that he had gone too far. "You can't go. We've got to talk this thing out together."

"To hell with your 'together,' man."

Paul grabbed Wally's arm.

"Together, Wally! Together!"

"Don't mess with me, man!" Wally wailed, yanking his arm away from Paul and turning into the hallway.

"Wally!" Paul called out. "If you go now, you'll regret it."

Wally was already out the front door. Paul considered running after him, but didn't want to risk a scene. All he needed was for someone like Elena Rothman to see him having an altercation with a patient in the street.

He went back into his office and collapsed at his desk. It had been a terrible twenty-four hours—beginning with the evening at Elena's, right straight through to the session with Wally. In many ways, of all the things that had happened in the last day, the incident with Wally was the most upsetting, for up until now, despite his growing troubles, Paul had been able to function effectively in his profession. Now he had broken one of the cardinal rules of psychiatry: a therapist never makes value judgments about what a patient says or does. At least, that was how it was supposed to be. But then, Paul thought, as he pulled the gold box from his pocket, nothing was the way it was supposed to be lately.

"I trusted the son of a bitch. I really trusted him. Do you know what it's like when you count on somebody, and then they dump all over you? Do you know what that fucking feels like, Frank? Do you?"

Wally Darrow sat on a bar stool, talking into his

gin on the rocks while a black barman did his best to ignore him.

"Hey, Frank! I'm talking to you. Why the fuck aren't you listening to me?"

"Because you drunk, brother," the bartender replied. "And that shit you been talkin' for the last half hour ain't makin' no sense!"

"Where the fuck am I, anyway?"

"I already told you, man. You in Newark."

"Newark!" Wally laughed loudly. "How did I get to Newark?"

"I don't know, man," Frank said, drawing two beers from the tap, "but I sure can think of a couple of good ways to get your ass outta here."

"How about giving me another one of these?" Wally asked, indicating his empty glass as Frank served a couple at the far end of the bar without acknowledging him. "Hey, Frank!" Wally shouted. "I said I wanted another drink. Why the fuck aren't you doing anything about it?"

"Because you drunk, brother," the bartender repeated, returning to where Wally was seated. "And I'll tell you somethin' else. If you don't shut your mouth, I'm gonna have to throw your ass outta this place. This ain't no trash establishment, you understand."

Wally laughed. "I guess you're trying to tell me that this dump has class!" he said, oblivious to the two large black men who now stood behind him. "Everybody wants to be so goddamn important. That's the trouble with this country. Everybody's so busy thinking they're such hot shit that they don't care about anybody but themselves. You know that, Frank? I mean, look at you. Here you are working in a nigger bar in Newark, New Jersey, and you think it's the goddamn big time—"

Wally didn't get a chance to go on with his speech because Frank had already nodded to the two men. With lightning speed, they grabbed Wally by the back of his collar and pulled him roughly across the barroom floor.

"Hey, what the fuck are you doing?" Wally protested. "Let go of me, goddammit!"

"We should beat the shit out of your white ass," one of the men said as they hauled Wally outside, "but you're too far gone for that. Just don't you be coming round here no more, you hear?"

"You dig?" the other man added, pushing Wally into the street.

Before Wally could reply, the two had disappeared inside the bar.

Wally looked back at the building, and then out into the street. He still had no idea how he had wound up in Newark, nor did he know what time it was. Probably he should go home, he thought. He saw a cab heading toward him and started waving frantically, but the vehicle sped past without stopping.

"Son of a bitch!" Wally shouted, holding up his middle finger at the cab.

Several seconds later, another cab appeared. This time, instead of just waving, Wally rushed out into the middle of the street. The cab had to swerve to avoid hitting him.

"What the hell's the matter with you? Are you crazy?" the driver, an elderly Jewish man, yelled out of the window, as Wally staggered over to him.

"Hey, mister. I need to get to Passaic. You gotta help me."

"I don't gotta do nothing, kid, except maybe call a cop. You coulda got us both killed back there!"

"No, please, you don't understand. I gotta get home," Wally pleaded and started to open the rear door of the taxi.

"What do you think you're doing, kid?" the driver demanded. "I don't pick up people off the street. I'm a radio car."

"Please, mister. Please!" Wally implored, climbing into the back seat. "Here, here's money," he said, taking a wad of crumpled bills out of his pocket. "You can have it all. Just get me to my goddamn house!" Wally shoved the money into the driver's hand. "Come on, mister, please! I gotta get home."

The driver unwadded the bills and counted them. "So let's take a ride to Passaic," he said, realizing that Wally had given him almost thirty dollars. "Where do you want to go?"

"Four fifty-seven Main Avenue," Wally answered. Then he passed out.

"Hey kid, wake up. We're here."

The driver had pulled up alongside a three-story brick building on a dark, treeless block. The lower floor of the building housed a delicatessen on one side and a thrift shop on the other. At the center, a set of cement stairs led to a rooming house on the second and third floors.

"We're here," the driver repeated.

"Huh? What the fuck?" Wally said, opening his eyes and shaking his head.

"This is where you wanted to go, kid. Four fifty-seven Main."

"Oh, yeah, yeah," Wally said, squinting at the brick building, trying to make the two buildings that appeared before his eyes turn into one.

The driver got out of the cab and helped Wally to his feet. "You live here?" he asked.

"Yeah," Wally answered, attempting to get his balance.

"Well, here you go, kid," the old man said, stuffing money back into Wally's pocket. "You need this a lot more than I do."

"What?"

"And do yourself a favor," the cabbie said before he got back into his car. "Lay off the sauce. You're too young. You know, I had a brother like you. He started when he was seventeen years old. We buried him before he was thirty. Take my advice, it's not worth it. That stuff ain't gonna get you anywhere. Except in trouble."

Standing on the steps of the rooming house, Wally watched the cab drive off and tried to take in what the old man had just said. Give it up. Lay off the sauce. Christ, Wally thought, it was always the same thing. Everybody always wanted to tell you what to do. If he wanted to have a drink, why couldn't he? Why didn't anyone realize that the reason he liked booze was that it was something you could count on?

As he staggered up the stairs to his room, Wally wished that he hadn't thrown away two bottles of gin the week before. It was all fucking Paul's fault! Paul, who had turned out to be like his mother, his teachers, his brothers—like everybody else he'd known in his life. Paul, who had called him a big overgrown baby. Paul, who had given him hope and who had then taken it away, who had once again proved what Wally had always known: it was a mistake to trust anybody—ever.

But booze, that was different. It never let you down. You could count on it to make you drunk, to make you hung over, sometimes to make you sick. But even when that happened, and you spent hours throwing up your guts, at least you knew what you were getting into. People weren't like that. With people, you never knew what to expect.

Reaching the door to his room, Wally heard the sound of the one other thing in his life that he could count on—his little shorthaired mutt Champ. The dog was jumping up and down inside, anxiously waiting for Wally to open the door.

"Hey, fella, how you doing?" Wally said. He picked up the dog and held it in his arms like a baby.

Thrilled to see his master, Champ panted and licked Wally's freckled face.

"Come on, fella, I bet you're hungry," Wally said, putting Champ back down on the floor and making his way to a cabinet that stood next to a small sink in one corner of the room. He took out a can of dog food, opened it, and emptied the contents into a dish. While Champ eagerly devoured his meal, Wally went back to the cabinet and found an unopened bottle of sherry. He had won it during the Christmas holidays at a Puerto Rican bar in Hackensack, and although he had thought about throwing it away with the gin, he had finally decided not to, thinking that he might give it to someone as a gift. He had even thought of giving it to Paul, as a sort of thank-you present.

He went through one glass quickly and was pouring a second when he felt Champ tugging at his trousers. Wally leaned down and petted his friend.

"You want to go outside and take care of business, don't you? Okay, fella," Wally said, getting up and taking Champ's leash from a hook on the front door, "let's go for a walk."

He put the leash on the dog and stumbled down the stairs. Main Avenue was deserted, and as Wally looked up and down the street, he felt that, in a way, it was good to be outside in the night air. He liked having the street entirely to himself. Just him and his mutt. With no assholes to spoil it. Yet, in spite of his feeling of contentment, Wally sensed that something was wrong.

It was Champ who noticed them first. A redheaded woman was walking a big German shepherd on the other side of the street.

"Settle down, fella," Wally said, as Champ pulled hard on his leash.

The woman and her dog were crossing and heading in Wally's direction.

"Stay on the other side, will you?" Wally shouted to the woman.

Champ and the shepherd had already started barking at each other.

"It's okay, fella, it's okay," Wally said to his dog, but the noise that the two animals were making was really getting to him. Soon the German shepherd was practically on top of Champ, and the barking became louder as each dog tugged on its leash and jumped at the other.

"Why didn't you stay over there?

"And why don't you go fuck yourself, mister!" the woman snapped back in a Spanish accent.

"Spic bitch," Wally yelled as the woman continued down the street.

Champ kept right on barking and snarling.

"It's okay, fella, stop it!" Wally said, not realizing that he was now screaming at his dog. The hysteria in his voice only made Champ bark louder. "Come on, fella, shut up now. That's enough, okay? That big mutt's gone now. Cool it!"

But the noise had already pushed Wally over the edge, and before he knew it, his hand rose in the air and came down hard across Champ's head. The little dog's barking turned into a piercing, high-pitched yelp.

"Stop that, man. You gotta stop that. I can't stand that. You gotta stop, man. Please!"

But there was no stopping Champ now.

"Please, man. Please!" Wally begged, unaware that he had picked up a board lying in the street. "Just fucking stop it!"

Champ's cries became even more intense. As if in a trance, Wally lifted the board over his head and with tremendous force slammed it down on the dog's skull. Champ's yelping crescendoed for a moment, and then there was silence.

Seconds passed, then minutes, before the bloody reality of what lay on the street registered in Wally's brain. When he finally realized what had happened, he dropped to his knees. Bending over and picking up the remains of what had been his friend, Wally made a sound that he hadn't known existed inside him—a low, wailing sound that came from deep within his being. His whole body shook.

Then came tears. How could he have done it? He hadn't wanted to. It was just like the woman in Beirut. He hadn't wanted to do that either . . . but she hadn't stopped screaming, and Champ hadn't stopped barking. What kind of monster had he become?

"Christ, help me," he sobbed, pressing the bloody carcass in his arms against his chest. Minutes ago, there had been just two things in his life that mattered—his booze and his mutt. Now, there was only one.

July 20

"I guess what scares me the most is that the dreams have started up again."

"Tell me about them," Paul said mechanically, more concerned with his own nightmares at present than with Joanna's.

"I fall asleep and it's happening all over again. He's there and the red carnation keeps getting bigger and bigger while he's forcing me to have sex. I wake up thinking I'm choking on it. Then I have this other dream where I'm in a field, and there are carnations growing everywhere, smothering me."

"When did they start?"

"After Dr. Abrams's death. I thought I had them licked. But now, it's like going back to square one. I came to look on Dr. Abrams as my only hope. If only he hadn't gotten sick—"

She shook her head and reached for a tissue.

"And now ... I ... oh, I'm sorry," she said blotting her tears. "I don't want to be crying all the time. God, I'm really sorry, Dr. Manning."

"It's all right," Paul said. "There's no reason to be ashamed of your feelings."

"But I must seem like such an idiot to you. And ungrateful."

"What do you mean?"

"Praising Dr. Abrams all the time."

"You're very upset, that's all. And with good reason."

"Yes, but what am I going to do? I feel so helpless."
She was crying even harder now.

Paul looked at the sad young woman facing him. He wanted to comfort her, to let her know that he understood her confusion, her torment. He was so tired of espousing the usual platitudes about letting feelings out, about how healthy it was to cry. If only he could do something to really ease someone's pain for a change. Without thinking, he stretched out his arm and took her hand.

"You're going to be okay," he said, gently massaging her fingers. His voice was the one he used with his daughter whenever she hurt herself playing in the garden. "It's all right, Joanna. Everything's going to be all right. Believe me, I understand."

He felt Joanna's hand tighten in his and watched her blush. Slowly, he got out of his chair and sat next to her on the couch. In a strange way, he was attracted not only to Joanna, but to her pain as well. Ultimately, it was a reflection of his own. She looked away, but he took her face in his hands and forced her to turn toward him.

"I don't think we should . . . be this close," she said, her body stiffening.

Paul stood up. He realized that he had let himself get out of control once again.

"I'm sorry," he said. "I didn't mean to make you uncomfortable." He moved over to his desk and leaned against it. "I only wanted you to feel better, Miss Harrison."

"Please don't call me that. That only makes me feel more idiotic."

"Idiotic? Why?"

"Because now I've offended you, and that's bad because . . ." Her voice trailed off.

"Because?"

She lay back on the couch and stared up at the ceiling.

"Dr. Manning, this is very difficult, but I know I'll hate myself if I don't say it now. So please excuse me. You see, when you sat down beside me a second ago, I was afraid. Really afraid, but not of you. I was afraid of me."

Paul nodded. He had a hunch about what she was going to tell him. It made him uneasy, but at the same time, he longed to hear it.

"You see, for months now," Joanna went on, "I haven't even let myself think about getting close to a man. Except that, in a way, I was close to Dr. Abrams. He was like a father to me. And then, all of a sudden, there was you. That afternoon I met you in the hospital, I felt something. I guess I recognized that perhaps I could be close to you, too."

"That's good, Joanna. Shows how far you've come."

"But not close like a father and daughter. With you, it was more . . . it was . . ."

Again, Joanna was silent. She looked at Paul, waiting for some signal from him as to whether or not she should continue. Paul made no move.

"I didn't want to be attracted to you!" she blurted out. "I didn't want it when I first met you, and I don't want it now. I know it's wrong, but I can't help it. I thought the feeling would go away once I started coming to you as a patient, but I was mistaken. Everything's only gotten worse. And then, when you held my hand and touched my face, I was terrified. Terrified because I wanted you to hold me . . . and I wanted to hold you, too." Joanna covered her eyes with her hands. "Please forgive me, Dr. Manning," she whispered, unable to look at Paul. "I'm so sorry. I really am."

"I forgive you, Joanna," Paul said softly, as he knelt down beside the couch where she lay. "It's not your fault. It's not anyone's fault."

He took her hands away from her face and kissed her on the forehead. Then on the eyelids. She shuddered and he kissed the hollow of her neck.

"Move over," he said gently as he again sat down beside her and took her in his arms. He was crying now, too. He couldn't remember when he had been so touched by another human being. It was overwhelming. He kissed her on the lips. It was a slow, open mouthed kiss that intensified the longing they felt for each other.

"This shouldn't be happening," Joanna said, while Paul started unbuttoning her blouse.

"You're right," he answered simply, slipping off his trousers and helping Joanna out of the rest of her clothes. Then he pulled her toward him again and they kissed passionately.

"Oh, God, it's so good," she sighed. "I didn't think it could be like this again."

"Me either," Paul said, looming over her, his penis huge and erect.

He took hold of her buttocks, pulled her to him, and started to enter her gently.

"Oh, no," she moaned.

"Yes," Paul said, as she relaxed and let him slip smoothly inside her. "Yes."

Their bodies moved together, slowly at first, then more and more rapidly. Everything seemed so simple to both of them. Everything seemed to make perfect sense. They each needed the other. Desperately.

As they started to climax, each hoped that the moment would last forever.

July 22

Sunday night. Joanna has just left. Spent whole weekend. Fantastic sex! So easy. So different from that bitch the other night. This girl really needs me. Treats me as if I'm this superhuman stud, too. Definitely want to see her again. And she wants to see me. Told her about Vivian and she seems to be able to handle it.

But can't continue to be her doctor. Will have to deal with this sooner or later. Too exhausted now to think about it. Forgot how tired good sex could make you.

Final note as I'm falling asleep. Darrow kid doesn't show up for his Saturday morning session. Just as well— since Joanna was here. Didn't even call. Know the game. Patient disappears, expects me to be concerned. Well, Paul isn't playing. No time now to worry about some kid who doesn't appreciate my true worth. Like someone else I know.

Are you listening, old man?!?

III.

July 27

Joanna had almost forgotten how wonderful it could be to go shopping in a big department store like Bloomingdale's. The crowds, the good-looking, well-dressed salespeople, and, most exciting of all, all the beautiful things to buy. As she admired the seemingly endless stacks of men's short-sleeved cotton shirts under a glass counter, she felt a rush of joy. Here she was, for the first time in over three months, actually braving a New York City department store and not feeling afraid.

"May I help you?" a young man with a mustache and short dark hair asked pleasantly.

"Oh, yes," Joanna answered, appreciating the man's smile and good looks—and not feeling threatened by them. "Could I see the green one with the stripe around the sleeve?"

"Of course," the man answered. "What size?"

"Oh, I'm not sure. He's a little bigger than you, I'd say."

"How about a large, then? You can always exchange it."

The young man smiled again and pulled out a shirt from under the glass. As he did so, Joanna wanted to hug him—for being polite, for being handsome, for smiling at her so magnificently. There really were men in the world who were all right, she thought. That was the wonderful breakthrough that she had finally made. Dr. Abrams had pointed her in the right direction, but it had been Paul who had taken her all the way—to the other side of her fears. Almost miraculously, someone meaningful had come into her life. Someone she could feel excited about, have pleasure with, buy gifts for.

Unfolding the shirt and holding it up in front of her, she pictured how Paul would look wearing it. Dashing Paul, with his broad shoulders, his blond hair. Paul, with whom, in just a few hours, she would leave to spend a glorious weekend at a beach house on Long Island.

"I think it will be fine," she said, returning the shirt to the salesclerk.

"Would you like it giftwrapped?'"

"Oh, yes . . . I never thought of that! I'd love it. Thank you."

Again she wanted to hug the young man, for his kindness and his understanding. It was as if he were an extension of Paul's kindness and understanding. As if, suddenly, her whole world were an extension of Paul. Life was so uncomplicated, so full of joy now. Now that she had fallen in love.

July 28

Mike Darrow pulled up alongside his brother's rooming house and shot a quick glance at the group of young men drinking beer in front of the grocery store across the street. He was convinced that they were eyeing him and his new BMW in a way that could only mean trouble, but he decided to take a chance and park there anyhow. As he got out of the car and locked the doors, he tried hard to appear casual and unconcerned, but inside he felt anxious.

Wondering how he always seemed to get dragged into his kid brother's misadventures, he headed up the steps of the seedy brick building. As he pushed open a door to a dimly lit hallway, the resentment he had been feeling grew even stronger. What was he doing, on this warm Saturday evening, standing in this squalid place that reeked of piss? Why had he left the barbecue that he and his wife had been having with their neighbors? What would his friends in Red Bank say if they knew that he, Mike Darrow, well-respected businessman and community leader, had a brother who lived a life just a step above Skid Row? For a moment he thought about turning around and leaving, but he couldn't—not when his mother had asked him, pleaded with him, to come here.

"Is anybody there?" Mike called, knocking on the door.

There was no answer, but he heard someone cough inside.

"Hey, Wally? Are you in there?" he shouted.

"Who the fuck's out there?" a raspy voice responded from the other side.

"Wally, is that you? It's Mike."

"Mike who?"

"Mike your brother. Come on, Wally, open up!"

"I don't got any brother, man. Go away!"

"Come on, Wally. I don't have much time."

"You never had any time! That was always your problem."

"Look, are you going to open up or aren't you? I don't want to play games with you."

Suddenly the door opened.

"Then why the fuck are you here?" Wally asked bitterly.

At first, Mike was too shocked by what he saw to answer. He had seen his brother strung out before, but tonight took the prize. Wally had lost a lot of weight, and since he was naked except for his shorts, it was painfully obvious. His red hair, now very long, was matted and filthy. His cheeks were sunken, his eyes bloodshot and lifeless. But worst of all was his smell—a mixture of stale alcohol, urine, and excrement.

"Jesus!" Mike finally said in disbelief. "What the hell's happened to you?"

"What the hell do you care?" Wally answered, staggering away from the door and falling back onto his bed.

Mike entered the room. "I thought you had quit drinking."

"I did." Wally laughed and took a swig of gin from a pint bottle by his bedside.

"Come on, don't give me any crap. When did you start up again?"

"None of your business."

"Don't tell me that, kid," Mike said angrily. "It is

my business—especially since you have Mom all upset again. She expected you for dinner today. You could have called her if you weren't going to show up. She hasn't heard from you in over a week and she's frantic."

"I don't have a phone."

"I guess you think that's funny, Wally. Well, let me tell you—"

"Before you tell me anything, let me tell you that I don't give a shit about what you think or what you have to say, Mr. Insuranceman! So why don't you just get out of here?"

Mike shook his head in disgust and frustration.

"What happened to that psychiatrist you were seeing? I thought he was supposed to be helping you."

"Not that asshole."

"Does that mean you're not going to him anymore?"

"You know," Wally laughed bitterly, "you're a fucking genius, man. You should be selling life insurance or something."

"Cool it, Wally. I haven't come all the way up here to listen to your lousy jokes."

"Nobody invited you here, so you'll have to listen to whatever comes over the air."

Mike tried hard to keep a grip on his temper. "How much longer do you think you can go on like this? Seriously?"

"Like what?"

"Living in this pigsty, drinking, not eating. You're wasting away, do you know that? You look like you're practically fifty years old. When's the last time you had a meal?"

"Who cares?"

"Mom cares."

"Bullshit!"

"You know, Wally, there are places for people like you."

"Huh? What are you saying?"

"I'm saying that, if you can't take care of yourself, we're going to have to step in and put you somewhere where you can be taken care of. Because, frankly, I've about had it with you, baby brother."

Wally did a slow burn. He pulled himself up from his bed and lunged at his brother. "Just get out of here!" he screamed. "I listened to your bullshit ever since I was born. I don't have to listen to it here. Get the fuck out!"

Mike pushed Wally back onto the bed.

"I've said all I have to say. Get your act together, or I'm coming back here with a doctor and a couple of cops if I have to. You've embarrassed us all long enough."

Wally looked at Mike accusingly. "Yeah," he said. "Embarrassed. That's it, isn't it? That's all you give a shit about—what your hotshot country club friends think."

"I'm giving you a week."

"A week? What do you mean, a week?"

"A week to quit drinking, for one thing. And to start going back to that guy you were seeing in New York."

"That asshole! Never!"

"One week." Before Wally could say anything more, Mike turned and walked out the door. He had already spent more time in the filthy rooming house than he had wanted, and when he reached the street, he was relieved to find his BMW still there and in one piece. If he hurried, and if the traffic weren't too bad, he might still be able to make it back to the barbecue in time for dessert.

July 29

The traffic on the Long Island Expressway was lighter than usual for a summer Sunday. Paul had figured it would take at least three and a half hours to drive from his Montauk beach house to the city, but as he neared the toll booths for the Midtown Tunnel, the clock on the dash of the Volvo station wagon said 8:30—a half hour earlier than he had expected. Joanna had been unusually quiet for much of the drive, and now lay asleep against Paul's shoulder.

"Sorry, honey," Paul said, nudging her gently as he pulled out his wallet to pay the toll.

"Are we here already?" Joanna said, still half-asleep.

"Afraid so."

"It was such a lovely weekend," she sighed. "I just don't want it to end."

"Maybe it doesn't have to," Paul said, giving her a sly wink as he drove into the tunnel.

"You mean—back to your house?" She put her hand on his knee.

"Why not?" Paul responded, excited once more by her touch, her eyes.

"Oh, Paul," she whispered, moving her hand further up his thigh. "This is so good."

"Yes, it is, isn't it?"

It had been good, Paul thought. They had spent the weekend at the beach just as they had spent the previous one in the city—mostly in bed. The only troubling incident had been on Saturday evening, when Joanna had surprised him with the shirt. He hadn't liked it and did a poor job of hiding the fact, and when she suggested that he wear it to dinner on the wharf, he somehow couldn't bring himself to do it. He knew he had hurt her, but he couldn't help it. Other than that, everything had gone well. Most of all, as he sped the Volvo down Fifth Avenue with Joanna snuggled next to him, Paul was thinking about and enjoying the return of his sexual prowess.

There was a small parking lot at the end of Paul's block, where many of the garden residents paid hundreds of dollars a month for the luxury of having a car in the city. The lot was guarded by a metal fence and a padlocked gate. As Paul approached it, he noticed another car blocking the driveway. At first he didn't recognize the car or the tall stocky man in a windbreaker trying to unlock the gate, but as he got closer he remembered the stockbroker from Elena Rothman's dinner party a week and a half ago. Then he saw Elena getting out of the passenger's side to help with the padlock.

"Christ!" Paul exclaimed.

"What is it?"

Without answering, Paul stepped on the gas and drove past the lot and out onto Houston Street.

"Why did you do that? Where are you going?"

"I think I'd better take you back to your hotel after all."

"Paul, sweetheart, you aren't making any sense. What's the matter?"

"The parking lot—one of the neighbors from the garden. It wouldn't look good."

"But couldn't we park somewhere else? What's wrong with the street?"

"Not safe." He pointed to the Volvo's radio/tape deck. "You're looking at one thousand dollars. It would be gone in ten minutes."

"Well, couldn't you drop me off somewhere?" she persisted, shocked by his sudden insensitivity. "Then you could park the damn car in your precious lot, and I'll meet you at your house in ten minutes."

"No, you don't understand. It's not safe. They could have seen you already."

"God, Paul! You sound as though I'm some sort of criminal."

He realized he was hurting her again. He didn't mean to, but he couldn't get beyond his panic.

"I'm sorry, I really am, Joanna," he tried to explain. "It was probably a bad idea, anyway. We should learn to leave well enough alone."

"But I want to spend the night with you, Paul. And you wanted to spend the night with me—a few minutes ago, anyway."

"Well, I changed my mind. Is that so terrible?" He was starting to get annoyed with her nagging, and now she was crying, too.

"Please, Joanna, don't," he pleaded, taking her hand. "Don't cry. The thing is," he went on, trying to spare her feelings, "we can't be together every night."

She continued to cry.

"We just have to go easy. One step at a time. You understand that, don't you?"

She said she did, but with little conviction. She sobbed quietly all the way to West Forty-seventh Street.

"I'll call you tomorrow," he offered weakly, once he had pulled up to her hotel.

"Okay, whatever you say," Joanna answered. They kissed good-bye, but with little passion or affection.

"And please," Paul added as Joanna was getting out of the car. "How about a little smile? Just for me. I don't like seeing those blue eyes all clouded up like that."

Joanna managed a faint smile, but Paul could tell she didn't mean it. He had hurt her and he couldn't undo the pain.

"God damn Elena Rothman," he muttered to himself as he shot the Volvo into Times Square. "God damn that bitch!"

Back on MacDougal Street, Paul was huddled over his desk, trying to finish his proposal for the restructuring of New York General's psychiatry department. After dropping off Joanna, he had returned to find a message on his answering machine saying that Alec Graham wanted to see him at the hospital the next morning. Paul was sure that this had to do with the chairmanship and that Graham was going to ask to see the proposal he still had not finished. As usual, the words weren't coming easily, and Paul kept crossing out practically every phrase that he wrote. Finally, he put the legal pad off to one side of his desk, got up, and unlocked the cabinet that contained his journal.

Can't write. Can't think. Joanna on my brain. This thing should not have happened. Getting too involved. Have to tell her how I feel. Sweet kid. Care for her—but not in love.

Have to find her another therapist. Fast. But don't want her divulging our relationship to anyone else in the profession. If Graham knew the half of it. Kiss chairmanship good-bye for good.

Paul awoke with a jolt. He expected to see someone at the edge of his bed, but instantly realized that the sound he had heard had come from downstairs. All was quiet now, but he was overcome with the feeling that someone had broken into his office. Easing slowly out of bed, he pulled open the drawer of the bed table and took out a small revolver. He tiptoed out of the bedroom and into the hallway.

From the edge of the stairwell, Paul could see that the door to his office was half-open. He was sure he had closed it before going to bed. Or had he? The desk lamp was still on. He was certain that he had switched it off. Or had he?

Gun in hand, Paul crept down the stairs. With each step, the dreaded presence that had awakened him grew stronger. His flesh tingled and his head throbbed as he came up on the half-open door to his office. He couldn't see anyone inside, but then, they might be lurking in a corner or hiding behind his desk or in the bathroom.

He had two options. He could storm the office or simply stand in wait and let the intruder reveal himself. Paul chose the former. He leapt into the room, hit the light switch, and made a sweep of the premises with the hand that held the gun.

No one.

The air-conditioner droned on indifferently as Paul now moved toward the bathroom. The door was closed. Instead of opening it immediately, something made him pound on it from the outside with his free hand.

"Come out, you coward son of a bitch," Paul shouted, slamming his fist wildly. "I know you're in there."

Nothing stirred. Exhausted, confused, and angry,

Paul finally flung open the door and turned on the light.

Again, nothing. Only his crazed reflection in the mirror above the sink.

He was very angry now. He was sure that someone had been there and was now playing tricks on him. Not only that, Paul was on to the mysterious visitor's identity. Before tonight, it had just been a feeling, a flash; but now, Max had invaded the sanctity of his home, with a vengeance, a force more powerful than Paul had imagined possible.

"How dare he," Paul said to himself, as he looked at the gun in his hand. "How dare he come here?"

He turned off the bathroom light and walked to his desk, where he put down the gun and picked up his journal. Usually, when he entered his thoughts, they were for his eyes only. This time would be different, however. Dramatically, Paul took up a pen and wrote in huge block letters.

YOU ARE GONE FOR NOW. BUT YOU'LL BE BACK. BE WARNED. WHEN YOU RETURN, OLD MAN, I'M GOING TO HAVE TO KILL YOU AGAIN.

July 30

Alec Graham sat down at his large oak desk and relit his pipe.

"Dr. Manning," he said in a quiet, controlled voice. "What I am about to tell you must be kept strictly confidential. Under no circumstances should anything I say to you go outside this room, is that clear?"

"Sure," Paul answered, wondering why Graham was acting so secretive for a job interview.

"Good." The chairman of the board of directors puffed on his pipe to make sure the tobacco had caught. "Now, as you may or may not know, an autopsy was performed on Max Abrams. There was no forensic reason for the procedure to be done. We all knew he was dying of cancer. Nevertheless, there's always the possibility that any autopsy we do can show us a little more about how to treat the living."

So that was it, Paul thought. It was the old man again. He felt something dreadful stirring in the pit of his stomach.

"In any event," Graham went on, "the autopsy showed nothing unusual. At least as far as Dr. Zimmer, our chief pathologist, was concerned. He confirmed what we all knew . . . that the cancer had spread to the vital organs and that secondary infection had set in, leading to respiratory failure. So far, so good. Or should I say, so far, nothing unexpected. Except for one thing. Dr. Zimmer was assisted the day he performed the post. One of our first-year residents was on hand to observe and to help with the procedure. He asked Dr.

Zimmer if he could run some additional tests, just for the practice."

"I see," Paul said, hoping his voice didn't give away the awful feeling he was experiencing.

"One of those tests did show something unusual."

"What was that?"

"A trace of a metabolite of succinylcholine was found in Dr. Abrams's tissue. The resident didn't think anything of it at the time. But later, when he showed Dr. Zimmer his findings, Zimmer came to me about it. To get to the crux of the matter, we've checked Dr. Abrams's records thoroughly, and found that he had never been given succinylcholine by anyone on our staff during the entire time he was a patient at this hospital. That means only one thing. Someone intentionally injected Dr. Abrams with the drug, and with enough of it to cause total respiratory paralysis. I'm afraid that what we're really talking about is not a very pretty subject. Euthanasia."

Paul nodded, but didn't say a word.

"Needless to say, Dr. Zimmer and I have been very quiet about all this. He hasn't even told the resident what I've just told you. Naturally, we don't want a word of this leaking out. I can just see the papers if they ever got hold of the story. They'd blow it all out of proportion and make it look as if euthanasia were standard practice around here. Still, we can't just sit back and ignore it either."

Paul cleared his throat and finally managed to speak. "Are you sure of the resident's findings? He could have made a mistake."

"I'm afraid not," Graham answered gravely. "Believe me, Paul, I didn't want to have to drag you into this. I'd just as soon that no one knew about it. In fact, I wish I didn't know about it myself. But I understand from Nora Hobson that you had visited him earlier in the evening."

"I did."

Graham paused and puffed on his pipe.

"Paul, did you notice anything going on between Miss Hobson and Max that night that struck you as peculiar?"

"I don't understand," Paul stated truthfully.

"This may seem farfetched," Graham explained, "but so far it's all I can come up with. Do you think it's possible that Max might have convinced Nora Hobson to give him the shot? She was there, she had access to the drug. Also, we all know that Max had a very persuasive personality. It might be hard for a nurse to refuse a New York General honcho . . . anything."

Paul breathed a secret sigh of relief. "But Hobson's worked here for over thirty years," he said, in full command of his voice again. "No matter who Max was, I can't see—"

"Paul," Graham interjected, "euthanasia is a very unusual crime. In fact, many people don't even consider it a crime. The perpetrator least of all. He or she thinks what they're doing is absolutely right, absolutely justified. So it's conceivable that Miss Hobson could have done this without too many scruples; especially if someone of Max Abrams's stature put her up to it."

Paul shook his head. "It just seems so unbelievable. The whole thing seems unreal."

"I agree. Unfortunately, as long as we have that damned lab report, it's all too real, I'm afraid."

"Have you spoken to Hobson?"

"Friday afternoon."

"And?"

"Not a thing. Between you and me, I don't think she did it anymore than I think you did."

"Where does that leave us, then?"

"Nowhere! That's the problem. To tell you the truth, I wish that the whole damned thing had never come up. I wish that Max Abrams had never had an autopsy, and that the resident had left well enough alone."

"Have you told the police?"

"No, not yet. I haven't told anyone yet. The only people who know about this are Hobson, Dr. Zimmer, myself, and now you."

"So what's going to be our next move?"

"Well, we do have one lead."

"A lead?" Paul felt his jaw tighten up. "What kind of lead?"

"It's probably nothing, but it seems that someone else went into Max's room after visiting hours were over that night—someone we're trying to get hold of now."

"Who?" Paul asked, his face feeling as if it had suddenly caught on fire.

Graham smiled apologetically. "I'd just as soon not say, Paul. The less anyone knows about this, the better at this point. It's probably just a shot in the dark, anyway. Unless, of course, it turns out to be the person who did it."

"And if it is?"

"You know as well as I do, Paul. If it is, then we've got a murderer on our hands. And as much as I don't like the idea, if there's anything suspicious about this individual, we'll have to inform the police and let them handle it from there."

"Well," Paul replied, rising carefully because his head was spinning, "if you need my help with anything, you know you can count on me, Alec."

"Thanks, Paul," Graham answered, standing up and showing Paul to the door. "Needless to say, you'll keep all of this to yourself."

"Of course, Alec," Paul said, deliberately avoiding shaking Graham's hand. His own had turned ice cold. "I understand . . . perfectly."

It had been a very bad day for Joanna. So bad that she had left her room in the hotel only to go downstairs and pick up a sandwich. Her sleep the night before had been restless. Finally, toward dawn, she had awakened screaming from a nightmare in which she was on a boat that was sinking in a sea of red carnations. She had tried to get back to sleep, but couldn't. As she lay awake, it upset her to think that a little thing like a dream could still affect her so strongly, especially since everything had been going so much better recently.

By noon, Joanna felt so anxious that she decided to skip her acting class. She had tried to read, but couldn't concentrate. All day long, she had been thinking about Paul, and had wasted a lot of time wondering when he would call. It was now almost nine o'clock, and she still hadn't heard from him. As she sat on her bed, staring at the telephone and willing it to ring, she thought again about his sudden decision to take her back to the hotel the night before and their awkward good-bye. She still didn't understand what had happened and wanted desperately to talk to Paul about it.

She got up from the bed and walked over to the window, once more resisting the urge to call Paul herself. An hour earlier, she had actually started to dial his number, but had hung up.

There were so many things she wanted to tell Paul tonight . . . how much she loved him, how much she missed him, how much she needed him. Then, too, there was the phone call she had received late that afternoon. One of the secretaries in the office at her acting school had phoned and told her to call someone named Alec Graham at New York General Hospital the next morning. Urgent! But Joanna had never heard of this Mr. Graham, and she wanted to ask Paul who he was, and what he could want with her.

She walked back to the telephone. Please, God, she thought. Please make it ring. Please let him be picking up the receiver and dialing my number right now. But the phone remained silent.

Traumatic day. Can't get over that Graham actually used the word "murderer." Also talked about calling in police. And I thought he wanted to see me about the chairmanship! Almost as funny as Nora Hobson being a suspect.

And who the hell's this mystery person who supposedly saw Max after visiting hours? Mr. X? And why has Graham omitted one other obvious suspect? Me. Or was he playing it cool to see how I'd react?

Why do I feel that I'm not alone as I write these words? Why do I feel that someone else is in this room—standing right behind me—looking over my shoulder? If I turn around now, I'll see—but if I stay exactly where I am—if I don't move, I'll be all right.

Must not turn around. It's—I can feel it breathing down

*my neck. IT! I can feel HIM breathing down my neck. You
want me to turn around and look at you, don't you, Max?
You want me to look you in the eye, you ungrateful bastard!
But I'm not going to, you hear? Remember what I told you
last night. Stay away, or I'm going to have to kill you again!*

The ringing of the telephone so startled Paul that he
dropped his pen. Shaking with terror, he let the machine answer for him.

"Hello, Paul?" Joanna's voice issued from the tiny
speaker on the machine. "I . . . I thought you were
going to call me today. I waited all day to hear from
you. I hope everything's all right. If you could give me
a ring when you're free, I'd appreciate it. I need to talk
to you about something. Thanks."

"But I don't need to talk to you," Paul said to
himself. His whole body was still shaking, and sweat
streamed from his forehead. Only a moment ago, he
had been sure that Max Abrams was in his office—not
far off, like the day on the squash court, not an image
on someone else's pendant, not in another part of the
house, like the night before, but literally right on top
of him. It had lasted only a few seconds. As he sat in
his chair, his eyes tightly closed, Paul waited in dread
for the old man's return.

When the telephone rang yet again, Paul was now
so absorbed by his fear of Max that he barely heard the
phone or Wally Darrow's scratchy voice.

"Doc, this is Wally. My brother wants me to come
see you again. Maybe he's right. I don't know. Anyway,
I was wondering if you had any time this week. I'll try
to reach you tomorrow at the hospital to find out. So
long."

Another voice from the past, Paul thought. First
Max, now Wally. What next?

July 31

Joanna turned away from Alec Graham and shook her head.

"I don't believe it," she said. "Dr. Abrams was dying. Why would anyone want to kill him?"

"To put an end to his suffering, perhaps?"

"But is that so terrible?"

"Terrible?" Graham reflected. "No, Miss Harrison, it's not terrible. But it is a crime, a very serious crime."

"It seems so silly, the way suicide being a crime is silly."

"It's still a felony, Miss Harrison, and we want to get to the bottom of it. That's why I've asked you here today. When Miss Hobson told me you were studying acting, I called just about every acting school in the city in order to find you."

"But how on earth can I help you?"

"Suppose I were to tell you that the drug that killed Dr. Abrams was not one that was given over a long period of time? Suppose I were to tell you that what killed him was a massive dose of something that acted almost instantly, a drug that Dr. Abrams had never been given before?"

"I don't know if I follow you."

"Simple. We wanted to speak to you, Miss Harrison, because the drug that caused Dr. Abrams's death was administered either right before you entered his room that night, or it was given to him while you were there."

Joanna looked alarmed. "You're saying that you think I did it?"

Graham shrugged his shoulders. "Not necessarily. There are a lot of other possibilities."

"Well, if there are," she came back angrily, "I'd like to know about them. It sounds to me as though you've got your case sewn up—and that I'm the guilty party."

"We haven't sewn anything up at all. I only wish we had. But I do have to ask you a few more questions. For instance, just how well did you know Dr. Abrams, Miss Harrison?"

Joanna perceived something ugly in Alec Graham's voice.

"I was his patient—and nothing more," she answered firmly.

"Did Max Abrams ever discuss his feelings about dying with you?"

"No, he didn't."

"Are you sure?"

"Of course I am. We never talked that much when I visited him. It wasn't easy for him to talk, and I realized that."

"Why did you go to see him then?"

"Because I missed him . . . and my sessions with him. I just needed to know that he was still there, even if he was dying."

"I see," Graham said perfunctorily.

"I'm not sure you see anything," Joanna said angrily.

"Miss Harrison, did Dr. Abrams ever ask you to help ease his pain?"

"He had me call the nurse a few times."

"What I had in mind goes beyond calling in a nurse. Let me be frank. Did he ever enlist your aid in ending his life?"

Joanna looked horrified.

"Well?"

"Never."

"You'd swear to that?"

"If I had to—yes."

"Then let me ask you something else. Did you notice anyone else in the area of Dr. Abrams's room the night you visited him? That room is a bit out of the way, if you recall. I think you would have noticed anything out of the ordinary going on in the vicinity."

"When I went into the room, he was alone."

"Not necessarily in the room, Miss Harrison. How about outside the room? You didn't by chance see anyone coming out before you went in? An orderly? A nurse? Anyone?"

"No, I don't think so . . . Only . . ." Her voice trailed off.

"Only what?" Graham asked eagerly. "Did you see someone?"

"The stairs . . ." Joanna spoke softly, as if thinking out loud. "But they wouldn't really be considered the vicinity of the room, would they? Anyway, he was probably coming from another floor."

Graham stood up and leaned forward across his desk.

"He? Who are you talking about? Did you see someone in the stairwell?"

Suddenly Joanna sensed that she had gone too far, said too much. All she could think about was getting out of this room, away from this awful man breathing down her neck. None of this would have happened, she thought, if she could have spoken to Paul the night before. Why hadn't he called her? Why hadn't he answered his phone? Where was he?

"Who, Miss Harrison? Who did you see?"

"I . . . I don't know," Joanna answered, feeling totally confused.

"But you just said you saw someone."

"Did I?"

"Yes, you did! You said you thought that he was coming from another floor. Who in God's name is *he*?"

"I . . . I . . ."

"Who?" Graham shouted.

"I don't know!" she screamed back before bursting into tears. "I don't know anything. I don't understand any of this. Why are you putting me through this?"

"Because a man has been murdered! And you obviously know something about someone who may be a prime suspect."

Murder? Prime suspect? What was this man saying? It was all too much. She had to talk to Paul before anything went any further.

"But you don't understand," she pleaded, getting a hold of herself. "It was just for a second. It all happened so fast that I only caught a glimpse of him."

"What did he look like, Miss Harrison? Surely you must remember something about him."

Joanna composed herself further. She knew now that the only way to escape from the room was to give a performance.

"He . . . he had dark hair," she said, finding it far easier to lie than to tell the truth. "And he was young . . . in his twenties, I'd say . . . on the short side . . . rather heavy."

"Good. Now we're getting somewhere. What was he wearing?"

"A T-shirt, I think."

"You think?"

"Yes," Joanna said carefully. "He was wearing a dark T-shirt . . . and jeans, I think. I told you I only saw him for a second."

"Can you tell me anything else?"

"I'm sorry, Mr. Graham. I've told you all I can."

"Well, Miss Harrison," Graham said, sounding relieved, "you've told me more than anyone else has so far. Now, are you willing to repeat all of this to the police if need be?"

"The police?"

Again, Joanna felt that she had gone too far. Lying to Graham was one thing. Lying to the police was another matter entirely.

"Well?" Graham asked, the aggressiveness returning to his voice.

"I . . . I guess I could . . . if I had to."

"Good. I'll be in touch with you, then." Graham thanked her and showed her to the door.

Joanna walked to a pay phone at the end of the hallway, found a quarter in her purse, and dialed Paul's number. She needed to talk to him now more than ever. There was just too much she didn't know, and whatever more there was to know she wanted to hear from Paul's own lips, but again all she heard was his recorded voice.

"God damn him," she said under her breath, slamming down the receiver. It was all his fault. If only he had called yesterday. If only she had been able to see him and talk to him before her meeting with Graham. Then none of this would have happened.

For a moment, she considered trying to look for him in his hospital office, or asking the page operator to reach him for her, but then she remembered Alec Graham. What if he were watching her right now, spying on her to see what else she might know, whom else she might be in contact with at New York General? No, there was only one thing to do, she thought, as she stood in front of the elevator bank, her finger on the down button. She would go to the Village and confront her lover in his home, even if that meant having to wait all night for him.

"How are you feeling now?" Paul asked. Wally Darrow had just recounted the story of Champ's death.

"Shaky," Wally answered, his voice barely a whisper. He was wearing a clean white shirt for his return to therapy, and his hair was combed as neatly as it had been for some time. Still, he appeared haggard, as if recovering from a long illness.

Paul was trying to act alert and interested in what Wally was saying, and the effort required was gargantuan. He had had a massive headache all day. Worse than that, his perceptions had been playing tricks on him. He kept having the feeling that if he looked at any one object for too long, something frightening might happen. Now, for example, he sensed that the colors of the orange and black print that hung on the wall across from Wally were more intense than normal—almost as if they were alive and smoldering with an energy that could burst into flame at any moment. Part of Paul wanted to investigate this bizarre sensation further, while something else told him that to do so was extremely dangerous. Paul was certain that the perpetrator of these visual tricks was Max. This was his latest way of taunting him and undermining his work.

Paul tried hard to return his full attention to Wally. He wondered how much longer he could keep up the facade of functioning as a therapist. Earlier in the day, he had considered cancelling all of his private patients. Now, he wondered if that might not have been a good idea. But that would have meant being alone in the house, and Paul didn't want that either. Ultimately, he had decided that his patients might protect him from Max and his pranks.

"You've lost weight," Paul said, as Wally came back into focus.

"Yeah, I guess I have."

"How come?" Paul asked, suddenly feeling that asking as many questions as he could was a good way to keep his own mind from noticing the menacing print lurking in the corner of his vision.

"Don't feel like eating all that much."

"Is that because you've been drinking?"

Wally nodded.

"When did you start up again?"

"When do you think?" Wally came back sharply. "It was the night I left here. The night Champ died."

"I see. Was it hard for you to come back?"

Wally didn't answer.

"I imagine that means it was," Paul said, no longer able to avoid the print. To his horror and amazement, the colors now seemed to be moving, swirling, bubbling.

"You really upset me, man."

"I'm sorry, Wally," Paul answered, trying to deny what was happening on the wall, wondering if he should terminate Wally's session then and there. "I . . . I had a bad day that day. I've been having a lot of bad days lately. I didn't mean to hurt your feelings."

Wally looked at Paul skeptically. "You really mean that, Doc?" he asked, his voice tremulous.

"I wouldn't say it if I didn't," Paul answered, blinking his eyes. He noticed now that Wally had started to cry. Miraculously, the print seemed to have calmed down.

"I'm sorry, too, Doc," Wally sobbed. "I just thought that you were pissed off at me for no reason. I mean, you didn't even give me a chance to explain anything."

"What do you say we forget the whole thing?" Paul suggested, relieved that the painting was back to normal again. "Let's just forget the last session ever happened."

"It did happen, though," Wally said, rubbing his eyes.

"Would you like to talk about it?" Paul asked, finding solace in his potential to soothe Wally.

"Some of it, yes."

"Which part?"

"Champ. I feel like it was my fault, and I'll never get rid of that feeling."

"Why do you feel like that?"

"Because I wasted him," Wally replied. "And I don't even know how it happened. All I know is he wouldn't shut up when he saw that other dog. He made me crazy."

"Like the woman in Lebanon?"

"Yeah. Only this time there wasn't any asshole lieutenant standing over me forcing me to do it. This time I did it all by myself."

"Not completely."

"I don't get you."

"You'd been drinking, hadn't you?"

"So?"

"Wally, we both know that alcohol can alter the personality."

"You mean that I killed Champ because I was plastered?"

"Let's just say that your being drunk had something to do with what you did. I think it's better to look at what made you take a drink that night, instead of talking about why you killed Champ."

As Paul spoke, he began to feel a new sensation. It was as if he were watching a scene from a play—a scene between a therapist and his patient. Paul was both the audience and the actor playing the part of the therapist. As audience, Paul was highly intrigued by his own performance. As actor, aware that he had an appreciative audience, Paul began to say his lines with even more commitment.

"How were you feeling the night you killed the dog?" Paul asked.

"Pissed off."

"Anything else?"

"Yeah . . . sad."

"How do you mean sad?"

"Sad because you dumped on me."

"And when you took that drink, did you feel sad or angry?"

"Both. For a while anyway. Then I don't know what I felt."

"So the drinks let you forget?"

"Yeah, more or less."

"What else do the drinks let you do?"

"What do you mean?"

"Wally, you said something important a moment ago. You said that after a while, you didn't know how you felt. Let's put that another way. You're telling me that when you drink, you don't feel anything. When you started drinking again two weeks ago, you were angry at me. So you got drunk and didn't have to deal with your anger. You were in pain, too, and the booze also took care of that, didn't it?"

"Yeah, I guess it did. What's the matter with that?"

"I think you can figure it out for yourself, Wally," Paul answered, amazed by how logical he was sounding. "What's left of a person when he can't feel anger, or fear . . . or joy, for that matter?"

"He's empty, I guess."

"Worse than that. A person who can't feel anything might as well be dead."

Wally gave Paul a panicked look.

"Shit, Doc, I don't want to be dead! You know that. But I can't help it. The booze . . . it's too much for me. I don't think I can get off it. Ever. Christ, take a look at my fucking hands. The booze is the only thing that'll keep 'em from shaking."

"Wally, the booze is what's making them shake," Paul said, rising to his feet and making his point by grasping Wally's hand with his. "Don't you see that? But we have the power to make those hands stop shaking, just as we have the power to stop your drinking."

"How?"

"It won't be easy," Paul replied, letting go of Wally's hand, "but we were getting somewhere before you left treatment. Do you remember the session when I hypnotized you and you remembered all about Lebanon?"

"Sure, how could I forget that?"

"Well, hypnosis isn't only useful in helping us remember things that lie buried in the unconscious. It's also very useful in helping to keep us from doing certain things. Things that we don't want to do because they're harmful to us. Smoking and overeating for example. And drinking, too."

"You mean you can hypnotize a person into not taking a drink?'"

"Not quite that—but we can make the experience of drinking so unpleasant that a person won't want to take one."

Wally looked puzzled.

"It doesn't always work," Paul went on, "and it's not an answer in itself. It won't tell us all the reasons why you drink. But I think we agree, Wally, that the faster you stop drinking, the better off you'll be."

"You think it would work on me, Doc?"

"Yes," Paul answered resolutely. "I think it would." He didn't say that he was beginning to feel wildly excited by the possibility of putting Wally under hypnosis another time, nor that the more he felt he could control Wally, the less power Max's spirit would have over his own. "So, Wally, do you want to have another go at it?" Paul asked.

"Sure, Doc. Why not?"

"Why not indeed!" Paul said, smiling as he got up, closed the drapes with a flourish, and then dimmed the track lights.

"Now, just relax," he went on, as much to calm his own highly agitated psyche as to comfort the troubled young man stretched out in the reclining chair. "Just close your eyes and picture a nice, perfectly peaceful place. Maybe it's the same place you thought about the other time we did this."

Paul watched Wally carry out his orders, and felt exhilarated. He hoped that Max was watching, too, seeing what a good and powerful therapist he could be when he set his mind to it.

"Your eyes are heavy, Wally. Your arms are getting heavy, too. Your legs are very heavy. Your whole body is very heavy. You are falling into a deep, deep, deep sleep."

Wally was breathing regularly and his hands had stopped shaking.

"I'm going to count to five, Wally," Paul said, enchanted, almost hypnotized, by the sound of his own voice. "When I reach five, you're going to be fast asleep, just like the last time. Do you hear me, Wally? You'll be in a deep and wonderful sleep."

Wally nodded his head slowly.

"One . . . you're very sleepy," Paul said, pumping even more energy into his delivery. "Two . . . you're falling into a deeper and deeper sleep. Three . . . you're almost there. Four . . . you're on the edge of the deepest sleep you've ever known. Five . . . you're fast asleep!"

Wally now sat so utterly motionless that it was hard for Paul to believe he was the same trembling creature who had entered his office a half hour ago. Paul wanted just to stand and look at him for as long as he could—in the way that a craftsman admires his handiwork—but he knew that he couldn't do that. He felt that to stop and take too much time with anything might invite trouble. The only way to keep Max at bay was through vigilance and constant action.

"You are now sound asleep," Paul intoned, "and

you will not wake up until I tell you. You can open your eyes now, Wally, but you will still be asleep. Go ahead, open your eyes."

Wally did as commanded.

"Okay. Now repeat after me, Wally. Paul is going to help me."

"Paul is going to help me."

"Paul is my friend."

"Paul is my friend."

"I will always be grateful to Paul."

"I will always be grateful to Paul."

"Excellent."

Paul walked over to the bookshelves and picked up a decanter of sherry and a large wine glass. The size and shape of the glass reminded Paul of a chalice, and for a second, he felt that he was twelve years old and an altar boy again. The only difference was that altar boys in his day were never allowed to touch the chalice. It contained the body and blood of Christ, and only the priest could hold the sacred vessel. Paul smiled as he poured sherry into the glass; then he walked over to Wally and held it in front of Wally's eyes.

"Look what I have, Wally," Paul said, as if talking to a child. "You like to drink, don't you, Wally?"

"Yes," Wally responded without emotion.

"Well, when you wake up, you're going to want to drink this, and I'm going to let you. But when you swallow it, it's going to taste very bitter. So bitter, in fact, that it's going to make you very sick. So sick you'll want to throw up."

Paul put the glass down on the table next to Wally.

"When you want a drink in the future, you'll remember the sherry and how bitter it tasted, and how it made you sick. Now, I'm going to count to three, Wally. By the time I reach three, you'll feel much better and more relaxed than when you first came here. Okay, here we go. One . . . you're waking up. Two . . . you're coming out of your sleep. And three . . . you're awake!"

Wally yawned. "Did you do it?" he asked, blinking his eyes.

"Do you mean, were you under?"

"Yeah, it seemed so quick this time."

"Don't worry, you did just fine. How do you feel?"

"All right . . . good."

Wally looked around the room, and then his eyes were drawn to the glass of sherry.

"Shit, Doc," he said, longingly eyeing the glass, "I feel kind of thirsty. Do you mind if I have that?"

"Not at all," Paul answered casually. "If you want it, take it."

"Thanks, Doc. Thanks a lot."

Wally picked up the glass and began to drink. Then he started coughing.

"Jesus, Doc, what the fuck is that?" he asked, putting the glass back down on the table. "It tasted . . . like shit."

"It's just sherry," Paul said calmly.

Wally's coughing became more intense and he clutched his stomach.

"Are you sure? I never tasted anything like that before!"

Paul shrugged. "Just sherry, Wally."

"Holy shit . . . I think I'm going to puke, Doc!"

"Here, better come with me, then," Paul said, helping Wally out of the chair and leading him into the bathroom. The room was lit only by a night-light.

"Fuck, I don't know if I can make it."

"It's all right. You're not alone. I'm here."

Paul patted Wally on the back as the young man started vomiting into the toilet. After a minute or two, Wally raised his head and looked at him.

"Jesus, Doc, I'm sorry."

"Here, rest for a second," Paul instructed, sitting Wally down on the clothes hamper next to the toilet.

"Christ, Doc, I don't know what happened. Did you put something in that drink?"

"No, Wally, I put something in your mind," Paul said proudly. He took a towel and moistened it in the sink.

"Huh? You mean the hypnotism made it taste like that?"

Paul nodded and continued smiling.

"No kidding, Doc? It's magic!"

"It will be like that every time you have a drink from now on," Paul said. He began wiping Wally's face with the cool towel. "You were worried about not being able to stop. But you know now that I can help you, don't you?"

"You know, it's really crazy," Wally said. "I mean, I came here tonight thinking that I hated you. But now, I feel . . . I don't know . . . I feel . . ."

"What, Wally? Grateful, perhaps?"

The young man looked up at Paul.

"I don't know, Doc," he said hoarsely. "I don't know what to think . . . or what to do."

The two men were as close to one another as they had ever been, and Paul saw something in Wally's eyes that he had never allowed himself to see before. But tonight was different. Special. Tonight, while Wally Darrow sat perfectly still, unable to take his eyes off his therapist's face, Paul knew he could no longer ignore the look of absolute devotion in the young man's eyes. He gazed down at his patient, and at last permitted himself to take in all the love that Wally was showering upon him.

He thought about how Max had been looking at him, too—how Max had been with him just last night. But Max's eyes projected something alien, something venomous. Now, suddenly, Wally's adoration was like an antidote, with the power to counteract Max Abrams's hate.

Easily, smoothly, Paul began swaying in place, his knee brushing lightly against Wally's hand. Wally closed his eyes. Then he cupped his hand around Paul's knee and squeezed gently, inching his hand slowly upward until he was caressing Paul's thigh. Paul tightened the muscles in his legs, helping Wally to experience the reality of his body more fully.

"It's all right, Wally," Paul said, putting his arm around his patient and pulling him closer.

Wally slid off the hamper and dropped onto his knees. His face nuzzled against Paul's trousers and he began to whimper.

"Ssshhh," Paul said.

Turning to the full-length mirror that hung on the door of the bathroom, Paul was elated by what he saw. Rays of light shot out from the mirror. The two men reflected in the glass were the image of something beautiful, something holy. The Prodigal Son was returning to his Father. The Sinner was begging forgiveness from his Lord. The Penitent was being granted absolution. Paul bent Wally's head back and traced the Sign of the Cross through his hair.

"Be humble, Wally," he said tenderly. "Be humble and God will always be merciful."

Then, convinced that he was about to be worshipped in the purest way imaginable, Paul guided Wally's face to his groin.

At last, it's all starting to make sense. To think that of all people, a pathetic creature like Wally Darrow has shown me the way. For it was when I looked into his eyes tonight that ALL was revealed. ALL that I AM! I know now that I am here for a reason. I have a mission.

Tonight I realize at last what I felt on the squash court and what I saw in the eyes of that little devil doll that Rothman had around her neck. And what I heard in my office. EVIL, Max, EVIL!

The night in your hospital room. The night when I acted out of goodness and mercy, I was negating everything that you stood for. Not as "Max," the physician I knew and worked with. "Max" was all an act . . . an intricately contrived cover to mask your true identity.

No wonder you're so intent on revenge. I should have realized from the start WHO you were and what you were up to.

And I should have seen all along that you were using her—to trap me! It was no coincidence that she was at the hospital—and at the funeral. You knew I couldn't refuse her plea for help, didn't you, Max?

But your final coup was engineering our sleeping together . . . to jeopardize my career, my marriage, my mission. She's your instrument for EVIL. But I'm on to you now and I'm going to fight back. There are too many people like Wally Darrow who need salvation. Believe me, Max, I'm not going to allow you to keep me from doing all the GOOD that I've been sent here to do. And SHE won't be able to do your dirty work any longer either. I'm on to everything now. And I shall triumph!

* * *

Joanna didn't leave the security of her window seat until a waiter asked her to move to a back table to make room for a couple who wanted dinner. For almost three hours, she had sat staring at the townhouse across the street, trying to summon up the courage to leave the cafe and go ring Paul's bell.

As she asked the waiter for the check, she thought once more about how she hated herself for being so timid. After all, Paul was her lover. She had every right to see him if she wished, and now was the time to do it. Nobody had gone in or out of the house for quite some time, not since the redheaded man had emerged, nearly three quarters of an hour ago. Paul must be alone now. Alone and perhaps trying to call her this very moment, to tell her that he was free and wanted to spend the rest of the night with her.

"Waiter, hurry please!" Joanna called out anxiously, convinced now that her lover was across the street trying to reach her.

The waiter glared. "Two lousy red wines in three hours," he muttered to himself, as he handed her the bill.

She paid the check, left a modest tip, and walked out into the muggy late-July night. Crossing the street hurriedly, she made straight for Paul's door and rang the bell. She tried to convince herself that the reason her heart was beating so rapidly was because she was happy.

A minute passed and the door remained closed. A worried look now came over Joanna's face. She rang again, determined to find out the truth, if it meant standing there all night. Another minute passed before she finally heard the inner door of the foyer being opened.

She was shocked when the outside door opened and she saw Paul up close. His hair was uncombed, his shirttail was hanging out, and his face looked changed. There was something bloated about it, and his eyes had taken on a frightening intensity. So frightening that something inside Joanna began telling her to run, while something else was urging her to fling herself into the arms of this wildly attractive man who could make love to her so magnificently.

"Paul, darling, are you all right?" she asked hesitantly.

He nodded mechanically.

"May I come inside?"

Again, Paul nodded, though he now feared her presence, suspecting that Max was using her visit for some venomous purpose.

"I'm sorry," Joanna said, entering the foyer. "I hope you weren't taking a nap."

"No, I was awake," he responded with little feeling as the two of them made their way to the living room.

"I was worried when you didn't answer the bell."

"I was finishing up some paperwork." He moved to the bar and poured himself a vodka. "Can I fix you something?"

"No, I've just had some wine, in the cafe across the street." She sat down on the sofa.

"What were you doing across the street?" he asked, not moving from the bar.

"I was waiting there."

"Waiting there?"

"Yes, Paul," she said, clasping her hands in front of her in frustration. "I was waiting to see you. I didn't know what happened to you. I didn't know if you were ill, or angry with me, or what. I just didn't know."

"I wasn't ill," he answered, suddenly hating the little-girl voice that Max had her using—the same soft and vulnerable voice that had trapped Paul the first time he'd met her.

"Did you forget that you promised to call?"

"No."

"I . . . I don't understand."

Paul put his drink down and moved out from the bar. He knew he couldn't put off what he had to do much longer.

"Joanna," he began carefully, "I feel I have to explain to you that some very unexpected things have come up. You see, I've been very busy, and—"

"But couldn't you have called?" she interrupted. "I would have understood."

He didn't answer.

"Paul, I thought something horrible had happened to you."

He looked at her and still was unable to respond. There was something in her huge child's eyes that touched him, even now. How could he tell her that he didn't want to see her again—that he couldn't see her again? If only he could just speak the truth. How much easier it would be if he could explain to her how Max was using her for his own evil ends. But he knew that he couldn't expect Joanna to understand anything so complex as his battle with Max.

He knew, too, that his very survival was at stake now. With this in mind, he began the difficult business of ending his relationship with Joanna.

"Joanna," he said softly, "I think we need to talk about quite a few things. Important things. You see, when you rang the bell before, I wasn't working like I said. I was thinking. Last night when you called, I was thinking then, too. I was thinking so hard that I didn't call you back. And all day today, I've been thinking. What it all boils down to is that it's wrong, Joanna. All wrong."

"What's wrong?" she asked, although she already suspected the worst.

"Us. You and I. We're what's wrong."

Pain registered on her face and she tried to hold back tears. Paul saw her emotion and fought against being moved by it.

"It's not that I don't want to keep seeing you," he went on. "It's just that it's all gotten way out of control."

"Is it something I've done?" she asked frantically. "If it is, tell me."

"No, it's nothing like that."

"Then what is it?"

"It's a lot of things. My wife, for one."

"Your wife? Why are you bringing her up all of a sudden?"

"Because I'm going to be meeting her very soon. When we come back to the city, it won't be as easy for me to see you."

"Paul, I'm prepared to live with that. We could work something out. People do all the time."

"Joanna, can't you see that it was wrong from the beginning?" he asked, becoming irked by her persistence. "That's why we have to end this thing while there's still time."

"This thing? You talk about it like it's some kind of disease."

"Maybe it is," Paul answered callously, aiming his words more at Max than at Joanna.

"My God, Paul! What are you saying?"

"I . . . I'm sorry," he answered, "but there's no use arguing about it. It happened, and it was good while it lasted—but now I feel I can't afford to let it go on."

"Oh, that's lovely!" she said, her voice now full of rage. "And what about me? What about what I can't afford? Especially now—after what you've done to me."

"Done to you? What do you mean?"

"God damn you!" she shouted. "How can you stand there and pretend to be so innocent? You almost make it sound as though I seduced you. When you know it was the other way around! You knew everything about me. I told you my life story. You knew what I'd been through, even that I was attracted to you. I was a pushover and you moved right in. I bet you do it with all your women patients! You're no better than he was!"

"He? Who? What are you talking about?"

"The animal who raped me! Because in your own slick way, you've done the same thing. You've used me. I should report you, just like I should have reported him! But the awful part is that I let you do it to me. Do you know that I even lied for you this afternoon? That's how much I trusted you. But you're all bastards—every one of you!"

Joanna was crying hysterically now, but Paul was too distracted by something she had just said to care.

"What do you mean, lied for me?"

There was something menacing in his voice, something that forced Joanna to stop crying and look at him. A strange, glazed look had come over his eyes. It frightened her, and her better judgment told her not to say anything more about her interview with Alec Graham that afternoon.

"Tell me what you meant," Paul insisted.

"Nothing. I didn't mean anything."

"Tell me!"

She began to tremble. "I . . . I saw a man . . . at the hospital this afternoon," she said. "A man named Graham. I was called in to see him."

"Graham? Why would Alec Graham want to talk to you?"

"Because of Dr. Abrams," Joanna answered. "I saw him the night he died."

Paul looked at Joanna in disbelief. What was she saying? He walked to the bar in an attempt to conceal his shock. "I don't get the connection," he said, his hands trembling as he poured himself another drink.

"They don't think Dr. Abrams died a natural death. Did you know that?"

"Yes, I did," Paul responded coolly. "But why is Graham bringing you into this?"

"Because Dr. Abrams wasn't the only person I saw that night."

"I still don't understand."

"I also saw you, Paul," Joanna said calmly. "You were going down the stairs outside Dr. Abrams's room."

Paul felt his head begin to spin as the full impact of Joanna's story hit him. The demon Max was far more clever than he had ever imagined. How perfectly he had masterminded the whole affair.

"I don't quite see what my being in a stairwell can have to do with Max Abrams's death," Paul managed to say, trying to appear unruffled. He wondered just how much Max had allowed Joanna to see that night in the hospital, and how much she had told Graham.

"I don't either, but Mr. Graham seems to feel differently."

"You told Graham you saw me?"

"No, that's just it. I didn't. I lied. That's how much of a fool I've been. I gave Graham a description of someone completely different. You see, the real reason I came down here this evening was to talk to you about that night, before I told them anything more."

"What is there to talk about?" Paul asked coldly. "Do you want to ask me if I killed Dr. Abrams?"

"I . . . I don't know. I don't know anything anymore. I should never have come down here. It was foolish of me." She started to leave.

"Where are you going?" Paul realized that he couldn't let her go until he found out how much she knew.

"Home."

He took a step toward her. "But you can't go, Joanna," he said. "Not in the state you're in. I can't allow it."

He reached for her, but she eluded his hands and slipped past him.

"Don't touch me!" she wailed. "Don't ever touch me again! Just let me out of here, or I'll scream. I'll go to the police!"

She ran into the hallway and out of the house. Paralyzed with fear, Paul stood in the hallway and tried desperately to figure his next move.

Before Joanna's visit, he had felt so strong, so able to handle Max. But now, despite his newly realized powers, Max still had the upper hand. Joanna's visit had forced Paul to face the ugly truth that Max might very well be on the verge of ultimate victory. Paul couldn't let that happen. But here it was happening! And all because Max had arranged for Joanna Harrison to see him that night in the hospital stairwell.

"God damn you, Max!" Paul started shouting, kicking the stairs in the foyer like a child having a tantrum. "God damn the two of you!"

IV.

August 1

Paul rubbed his eyes. The spotlight distorted his vision. Next to him at the podium, his father, long dead, handed him a large package wrapped in shiny gold paper. Then, the crowd in the auditorium started chanting. "Go, Paul, go! Go, Paul, go!"

Paul felt a wave of panic come over him. He knew that the chairmanship of the psychiatry department was a very important position, and the doctor so honored always had to unwrap the package himself. But it was tied with yards and yards of cord and seemed so big, so impossible.

Out of the corner of his eye, Paul caught sight of a scruffy old man, beckoning to him from the wings.

"I'll help you, son," the man stammered. His breathing was labored.

"Will you, Max?"

"Sure," Max answered, savagely tearing at the wrapping of the package. After a few seconds, he tossed Paul his prize.

"Put it on, Paulie," he taunted.

When Paul saw what he was holding, he felt that there had been some mistake. Surely, this couldn't be what he had worked so hard for.

Again, the audience started shouting up at the stage.

"Put it on, Paul! Put it on, Paul! Harder, harder!"

Paul turned his back to the crowd, but there was no escape. Standing before him was Joanna.

"Put it on, you bastard!" she cried. Behind her

stood Alec Graham, as well as various members of the board of directors of New York General.

"You used me!" Joanna shouted. "You're no better than the animal who raped me."

With that, she grabbed the oversize artificial penis from Paul's hand and held it up to Graham and the board.

"You see how he used me! Take him! Arrest him!"

Suddenly, the board of directors were dressed in storm trooper uniforms, and they had a new leader—Max Abrams.

"My God, my God, why hast Thou forsaken me?" Paul cried out as the thugs started closing in on him. Their arms soon encircled him, and he knew that the end had finally come.

Paul closed his eyes. When he opened them again, the storm troopers' arms had turned into the branches of trees, and Paul saw that he was in a forest. It was very quiet now.

Suddenly, however, the sound of a gunshot ruptured the silence.

"I didn't mean to kill her," Wally Darrow said, his voice echoing across the forest. "I didn't mean to kill Champ either—but they wouldn't stop screaming."

Paul looked at the young man kneeling at his feet.

"I forgive you, Wally," he said, his attention riveted on the gun that was still smoking in Wally's hand.

"Thanks, Doc," Wally answered. He lifted the hem of Paul's flowing white robe to his lips and kissed it.

Sunlight flooded the scene and there was applause. Paul realized that he was back on stage. Behind him, the ending of a Biblical epic was being projected on a large screen. Superimposed over the scene in huge red letters the word THERAPIST appeared. As Paul stared at the screen, the letters began shimmering, then dancing, coming apart to form two words.

THERA PIST . . .
THER A PIST . . .
THE RAP IST
THE RAPIST

Paul watched, mesmerized. Slowly the letters dissolved into a gigantic, blood-red blur. Then, the outline of a flower became clear, an enormous flower—an enormous red carnation.

As the screen went black, a woman's screams filled the air.

Paul looked down at the red carnation in the buttonhole of his lapel and smiled.

When he awoke, Paul felt an amazing calm. It was as if all the torment of Joanna's visit had been shattered by the bullet from Wally's gun. Once again, Paul felt that he had the power to do anything. Thanks to his dream, Paul now knew exactly what he needed to do in order to defeat Max and make the world a safer place.

He looked at the alarm clock on the night table. It was still early—just a little past one-thirty. One of the first things he needed to do was to call Joanna. But should he do that now or wait until the morning?

He raced through all the times he had been with her over the last month. As far as he could remember, only the day of Max's funeral needed to be taken care of, the day Paul had given her his name and phone number and she had put it in her address book. Perhaps it was foolish to worry over such a small detail, he thought, as he got up and walked downstairs. Just the same, it wouldn't hurt to clear it up if he could. And why not do that as soon as possible?

Before picking up the phone in his office Paul double-checked his appointment book and saw that Wally Darrow was scheduled for a 6:40 session the next evening. Good, Paul thought, he could leave well enough alone there. He was convinced that Wally wouldn't cancel. It would be like cancelling an audience with the Pope.

Paul dialed Joanna's hotel and a clerk answered gruffly.

"Miss Harrison's room," Paul said, unconcerned that he had awakened the clerk. After several rings, Joanna picked up the phone.

"Hello?" she said, her voice heavy with sleep.

"Joanna," Paul said softly.

"Who is it?"

"It's me . . . Paul."

Seconds passed before there was a reply.

"Why are you calling?"

"Because of this evening. Because of the last few days. I'm calling to apologize. I don't know what got into me, darling. I just haven't been myself lately. I don't understand myself what it's all about."

"Well, it's too late."

"I didn't expect you to listen. You have a perfect right not to—but I wanted to tell you just the same. Believe me, Joanna, the last thing in the world I wanted to do was to hurt you. I'd rather hurt myself."

"But . . . why are you telling me all this? Why now?"

"Because I love you, Joanna," Paul said slowly. "I love you very much. Don't you see? That's why I wanted to end it tonight, because I was afraid. Afraid of what could happen. When I said things had gone too far, that's exactly what I meant. It's terrifying when you feel something this strong. That's why I wanted to run away."

"Oh, God!" she said. "If only I could believe you."

"You've got to, darling, please! I can't think of anything but you—and that frightens me. It frightens me to be so obsessed that I can't even do my work anymore. Somehow, I thought it would be better and less painful for both of us if you didn't know how I really felt, but when I saw how badly you took it, how much you love me, too . . . well, I knew I had to tell you the truth. I've been up all night wondering whether to call you and explain it all to you. I hope I've done the right thing, that's all."

"The right thing? Oh, Paul, if you only knew what I've been through myself tonight. Ever since I left you, I've felt like I wanted to die. When I came back to this room—"

"Joanna?" Paul interrupted, changing the pitch of his voice slightly. "I'd like to see you tonight. There's so much to talk about—now that things are out in the open. If we could be together tonight, it would mean a lot to me."

"Tonight? But—"

"I know it's very late," Paul put in quickly, "but I'd still like to see you."

"But . . ."

"I could come up there, if you want."

"No, it's horrible here. I don't ever want you to see this room."

"How about coming back here, then? You could be here in ten minutes."

"I'm not dressed. I couldn't get there before . . ."

"That's all right. I won't sleep tonight, anyway, not the way I feel. It doesn't matter what time you get here. All I know is that I don't think I can live without you. I was afraid to tell you that earlier, but I'm not afraid to say it now."

"Oh, darling, I can't live without you either," Joanna responded, starting to cry. "I can't believe I'm actually saying it . . . but I am. I need you so much. I love you so much."

"Please come," Paul said once more. "We have a lot to talk over."

"I know we do, darling. It's just that I . . . I don't want to be a fool again, that's all."

"If anyone's a fool, I am. Please come, please. I need you tonight, Joanna. Very badly."

"Oh, darling, I need you, too."

"You'll come, then?"

"Yes. Oh, God, yes! I'll be there in half an hour."

"I'll be waiting for you, darling."

Paul hung up the phone. Everything seemed to be going brilliantly, he thought, and it made him feel warm and peaceful. He glanced at his appointment book one more time. If only Wally Darrow had a telephone, then he could be sure of everything.

It was a little after 4:00 A.M. when Paul released Joanna and rolled over to his own side of the bed.

"Joanna?" he called in a low voice.

She was fast asleep and didn't answer.

"Joanna?" he repeated, a little louder.

When she still didn't answer, Paul quietly got out of bed and walked to the chair by the bedroom window where Joanna had left her clothes. Carefully, he pulled her handbag out from under her slacks and blouse. Then he crept toward the bathroom, holding the bag to one side, so that Joanna wouldn't be able to see it if she were to wake up unexpectedly.

Once inside the bathroom, Paul closed the door and turned on the light. Standing in front of the sink, he opened the handbag. There wasn't much inside: a wallet, hairbrush, chewing gum, bottle of aspirin, a toothbrush, and a well-worn address book—a tiny looseleaf book with a paisley canvas-covered binding. Removing it, Paul turned to the M's and found his own name, address, and phone number on the second page. Seeing that Joanna had doodled "Paul Manning" all over the page made him smile. It was as if a teenager had written the name of her latest heartthrob in her school notebook.

It was unfortunate, Paul thought as he tore the page from the book, that Max had picked on such a nice kid to do his dirty work. Somehow, it didn't seem fair. But it was too late now. There was no turning back. Still, he couldn't help feeling sad. She had been so excited an hour earlier when Paul had asked her to have dinner the following evening at a French restaurant uptown, and it had been touching when at first she had refused the invitation, claiming she had nothing to wear. But then he had kissed her and told her again how much she meant to him and she had agreed to go with him wherever he wanted, admitting that she had never been happier in her life.

Poor Joanna, Paul thought. So vulnerable, so trusting, so easily controlled. He had even been able to convince her that he and Vivian were on the verge of a divorce. And when he'd told her that indeed it was he who had given Max the fatal shot of succinylcholine, she had cried. Not out of horror, but out of empathy, because Paul had told her that Max had begged him to do it. She was going to stick to her story about having seen a short, dark-haired man in his twenties going down the stairs the night of Max's death.

It had almost been too easy, Paul thought. So easy that he had considered leaving well enough alone, but then he recalled the power of her anger earlier in the evening, and her threats. Not to mention the power of Max's continuing hold on her. Once again, Paul realized that what he was doing was not only right—it was the only thing he could do.

"Darling," a soft voice called from the bedroom, "are you all right?"

Paul stiffened.

"Of course I am," he answered. "I thought you were asleep."

"I woke up and missed you. You're not sick or anything, are you?"

"No, I'm fine. I just had to go to the bathroom. Why don't you go back to sleep."

"I can't. Not until you're beside me."

"I'll be right there," he answered, crumpling the page from her address book and flushing it down the toilet. "Want to play a game?" he said, as he ran water in the sink to muffle the sound of Joanna's handbag being snapped shut.

"What kind of game?"

"Close your eyes, and I'll surprise you!"

"At four in the morning? Paul, you can be so crazy sometimes!" She laughed.

"Go ahead. It'll be fun. Close your eyes."

"All right, if you say so."

"Got them closed?" Paul asked, slipping out of the bathroom, trying as best he could to conceal the handbag.

"They're closed, but hurry, darling. I want you in bed with me."

"I'm coming . . . but no peeking!" he said. He placed Joanna's bag back on the chair, approximately where it had been before. Then he walked to the bed and stood looking down at her.

"Okay, now don't be shy, open your eyes and you will have a big surprise!"

Joanna did as she was told. The sight of Paul's naked body and erect penis silhouetted against the window thrilled her.

"Oh, Paul, darling. Come to me now!" she sighed. "Don't ever leave me again."

"I won't, Joanna. I won't," he answered, taking her in his arms. "I'll be with you like this forever."

They made love one more time. For Paul, it was the most satisfying time they had ever spent in bed together. Knowing that it would never happen again, he felt a freedom he had never known before. For the first time, there was nothing to lose, nothing to live up to the next morning, the next evening. He allowed Joanna to experience the divinity of his body and spirit to an extent that he hadn't thought possible. If only it could always be like this, he thought, at the height of their pleasure.

When it was over, however, Paul realized that this

was nothing compared to the even greater freedom that lay within his grasp. The freedom and peace that Paul had known after Wally had shot the gun in his dream would soon be his. Only a few more things to take care of, and he would have it all.

"What are you thinking about, darling?" Joanna asked in the silence left by their lovemaking.

"Oh, nothing, sweetheart."

"You must be thinking about something."

"It's a secret," Paul replied, knowing that Joanna could never understand the new life that his dream had granted him.

"Come on, darling . . . please! Tell me!" she kidded.

"Tonight, when I pick you up for dinner—I'll tell you then."

"Okay," she answered, kissing his forehead. "I'll wait—if I have to. But don't be late."

"Of course not, Joanna," he whispered, embracing her once more. "I'll be right on time."

Paul Manning stood by Max Abrams's grave in Mount Sinai Cemetery. It was late afternoon and the place was deserted.

"After all your visits lately, old man," Paul said, "I thought I'd pay you one for a change. You know, I was afraid that you had the better of me for a while there, but I came through in the end, and soon I'll never have to fear you again. I wanted to make sure you were aware of the fact. That's why I came here. Also, I wanted to dedicate this special night to you, since you're the one responsible for it all. But don't expect me to share anything with you ever again. This is good-bye, old man. This is forever."

Paul threw a bouquet of red carnations on Max's grave, strolled back to his Volvo, and roared off to Manhattan.

"I'm glad you came," Paul said, closing the door to his office as Wally Darrow sat down in the familiar black leather chair.

"You okay?" Paul asked, also taking a seat.

"Yeah, I guess so," Wally answered faintly. "I couldn't sleep last night. I feel pretty wiped today."

"How come?" Paul asked, part of him wanting to reprimand Wally for not being exhilarated to be back in his presence.

"On account of I . . . I've been thinking that maybe there's something wrong with me."

"Because of last night?" Paul tried to sound dispassionate and professional despite his disappointment over Wally's mundane interpretation of the events of the previous evening.

"Yeah, Doc. You guessed it."

Paul had expected Wally to exhibit some confusion about his last session, and had rehearsed exactly what to say to put his disciple at ease. When he spoke now, it was with confidence and authority.

"Wally, let me assure you that just because something like that happens, it doesn't mean that you're gay. Remember, I had a part in what went on, too, and believe me, I'm not a homosexual. Never have been. I'm a married man with two kids."

"Then why did it happen?" Wally snapped back.

"It happened," Paul answered dramatically, "because you needed to thank me, Wally. For making you whole. Believe me, I know what I'm talking about. Last

[175]

night had nothing to do with homosexuality. What you did was beautiful, Wally. You were thanking me in a way that was pure and loving and, above all, manly. Manly, Wally . . . manly."

"Then why do I feel like a piece of shit?" Wally asked bitterly.

"That's easy enough to figure out. Don't you realize what you're doing? We're seeing a classic example of Wally Darrow dumping all over himself when given the slightest opportunity. You're being weak again. When you feel weak and no good, you take it out on yourself. It's a vicious cycle, and you know what the next step is as well as I do. Before you know it, you'll be hitting the bottle again, then blaming yourself for being a drunk, and the whole process goes on and on! Is that what you want for yourself, Wally? Is it?"

"No!" Wally shouted, before breaking into tears. "Fuck, no! I want to be something in this goddamned world. But how can I, Doc? It's too fucking hard."

"Nobody ever said it would be easy, but you can get better, Wally. I can make you better."

"How, Doc?"

"You were making progress in your therapy. Why take two steps backwards every time you take one forward? Don't you see that you're not a homosexual, Wally? You have a drinking problem, and an even bigger problem in terms of the way you look at yourself. You're so used to seeing yourself as worthless and no good that *you* believe it more than anybody else. We've got to change the way you feel about yourself, Wally."

"But how?" Wally asked, wondering why Paul had gotten out of his chair and was walking to the window.

"So far, Wally," Paul answered, closing the drapes,

"we've accomplished a great deal through hypnosis. I can't see any reason to stop using a method that's worked so well up until now."

"Hypnosis? Again, tonight?"

"Why not? You trust me, don't you?"

"Sure, but . . ."

"Just relax, Wally. If nothing else, it will help calm your nerves. All I want to do this evening is put some positive self-images in your mind. I want to help make you strong, Wally. I'll also show you that your fears about last night are totally unfounded."

"You can do that, Doc?"

"There are all sorts of things we can do, Wally," Paul said, giving him a locker-room pat on the back. "Just try to relax. Think of that nice peaceful place that you always go to. That place where nobody can bother you, where you're completely relaxed, completely safe."

The soothing power of Paul's voice was already getting to Wally. For the first time in twenty-four hours, he felt the tension that had ruled his body start to diminish. Paul dimmed the track lights.

"There's nothing to worry about, Wally, nothing at all. And, as always, there's so much to be gained. Just sit back and relax. Close your eyes if you like, you'll be a lot more comfortable with your eyes closed. Nothing can bother you at all, then. Nothing can keep you from feeling relaxed and good. I'm going to make you well, Wally. I'm going to heal you."

Wally's eyes were closed now, and he was breathing deeply.

"That's it, Wally. Let those eyelids have all the rest they need. After all, you haven't slept for a long

[177]

time. You're very tired and you need sleep very badly. Now, I'm going to count to five, Wally, and as I do, you're going to find yourself in a deep, relaxing sleep, just like the other times we've done this. Only this time, the peace you'll experience will be even greater than before. It will be so great that you won't even remember being hypnotized, Wally. You won't be able to remember any of this at all.

"Okay, here goes. I'm going to start counting now. One . . . you're falling deeper and deeper into sleep. Two . . . you're sleepier than you've ever been in your life, and it feels good. Very, very good! Three . . . you're already fast asleep, but you can go even further. Four . . . you're almost there. And five! You've made it, Wally. You've made it!"

Paul walked over to Wally, who now sat motionless in his chair.

"Do you hear me?" Paul asked, bending down in front of his subject. "If you do, nod your head."

Wally's head moved forward and then back.

"Good, Wally. That's very good," Paul said, unlocking a bookshelf cabinet and withdrawing a long package wrapped in gold foil paper.

"Now, as I've said, Wally, when you wake up, you'll remember none of this. All you'll remember is that you came here for your session, and that we talked for a while, and then you fell asleep. That's how tired you were.

"There's just one other thing, one minor detail. Before you wake up, I have a favor I'd like to ask of you. It's something that you'll have no trouble doing. It's very simple, really. Do you see this package that I'm putting down on the table next to you? All I want you to do is to deliver it to a young woman. She lives at the Stafford Hotel on West Forty-seventh Street. She's in Room 813. She's expecting someone at eight o'clock, so you should get there closer to quarter to eight. There's a coffee shop downstairs and you can wait there if you're too early. It's easier to get upstairs through the coffee shop, because you won't have to go past the desk clerk. Try to avoid the desk clerk if you can. It will make things much simpler. Since you can go right to the elevator from the coffee shop, no one will have to know you're delivering the package at all.

"Now, I'll tell you again what I want you to do, Wally. I want you to go to her room—Room 813—and deliver the package that's next to you. But Wally, and this is important, make sure the package is opened in your presence. That's very important, Wally. You mustn't leave until she opens the package. You see, it's a surprise, and I want to make sure she enjoys it. Do you understand?"

There was a barely noticeable movement of Wally's head.

"All right, now. I'm going to wake you up. When you're awake, you'll feel extremely relaxed, but still sleepy. So sleepy that we'll decide to end the session early so that you can go home and get some sleep. That will be perfectly all right, Wally. I realize how tired you are. But remember, you have to deliver the package first. After you do that, you'll be able to get all the rest you want. You'll be able to get all the rest in the world, if you like."

As Paul spoke, he opened the drapes and turned the lights back up.

"Now I'm going to count to three and snap my

fingers," he continued, returning to his seat opposite Wally, "and when I do, you're going to wake up. Okay? One . . . two . . . three!"

Paul snapped his fingers. Instantly, Wally opened his eyes and squinted at the light.

"Hey, that was some nap you took," Paul said in a friendly voice.

"What?" Wally asked, rubbing his eyes.

"You passed out. I guess you needed to. Are you okay now?"

"Yeah, I think so," Wally answered, yawning.

"Maybe we should call it a night?" Paul suggested.

"Okay, yeah. I mean, is that all right?"

"All right by me, Wally."

"Shit, I'm sorry, Doc. I didn't know I was so tired."

"No problem," Paul said, getting up. "I'll see you Friday."

"Sure, Doc. Friday," Wally answered, and also stood up.

"As a matter of fact, I'm not going to charge you for the session."

"You don't have to do that, Doc. It's my fault. I'm the one who fell asleep."

"No, that's all right. To tell you the truth, I'm pretty tired myself tonight. Let's just call it even, okay?"

"Okay, if you say so."

Wally started for the hallway. Halfway there, he stopped and looked around the room.

"What is it, Wally?" Paul asked casually.

"I . . . I don't know. I feel like I forgot something."

"Oh?" Paul looked at Wally and then pointedly at the foil-wrapped package on the table next to Wally's chair. "Is that what you forgot?"

Wally stared at the package. "Yeah," he answered vaguely.

"Well, it's good you didn't forget it then," Paul said, picking up the package and handing it to Wally.

"Thanks, Doc," Wally said. As he followed Paul into the hallway, he looked confused.

When they reached the front door, Paul put his hand in his pocket and pulled out a ten-dollar bill. He handed it to Wally and smiled.

"Now you go home and get some sleep, Wally."

Wally looked blankly at the money.

"What's that for?"

"That's for a taxi. You'll get uptown faster if you take a cab."

Zombielike, Wally took the money and put it into his shirt pocket.

"Thanks, Doc," he said as Paul opened the front door for him.

"Think nothing of it, Wally." Paul patted him on the back another time. "So long . . . and good luck!"

"Good luck? Why good luck?"

"Oh, I don't know. It's something we can all use a little of from time to time."

"Yeah, I guess so," Wally said as he started to walk up the three steps that led to MacDougal Street. "So long, Doc."

Paul closed the door. Standing in the foyer, he observed Wally through one of the little windows outlining the front door. Wally staggered slightly as he tried to accustom himself to being in the street. For a second, Paul worried that the young man might not be able to handle getting a cab, but then one turned from Bleecker onto MacDougal and Wally flagged it down and got inside.

When the cab had driven to the end of the block and turned onto Houston Street, Paul went back inside his office. He looked at the clock on his desk. It was 7:27. It would take Wally about ten minutes to get to the hotel. So far, the timing was perfect.

Next to the clock lay a postcard with a view of the Acropolis. It had arrived from Vivian that morning. Paul smiled to himself, picked up the card, and sat down in his reclining black leather chair. Adjusting the chair to a comfortable position, he lay back and toyed with the card. Now, all he had to do was wait.

As Wally entered the coffee shop of the Stafford Hotel, he thought momentarily about having a Coke or a cup of coffee, but when he noticed that the clock behind the counter said 7:40, he decided against it. Besides, he didn't really want anything anyway. All he wanted to do was to get rid of the shiny package that he was holding so carefully in his hand.

At the far end of the restaurant, a swinging door led to the hotel lobby. Wally headed for the door, opened it, and passed through to the other side. The lobby wasn't crowded—only a man at the desk talking with a young couple who seemed to be asking directions. Wally thought of going over and asking where Room 813 was, but something inside him told him to avoid the man at the desk at all costs and go straight to the elevator. Wasn't that why he had come into the hotel through the coffee shop in the first place?

Wally stepped into the elevator and pushed the button for the eighth floor. There seemed to be a lot of rules to pay attention to tonight, he thought. Somehow, even though he was aware of the rules, he didn't question them. Nor was he confused by them. What he was doing felt completely natural, completely logical. It was very simple—he had to deliver a package to a girl in Room 813. That, in turn, would free his hand of the package and allow him to go home and get some rest. Getting rest was the important thing now. The package was the means to that end.

When the elevator reached the eighth floor, Wally got out and looked up and down a long hallway broken by a number of identical blue doors. Now, all he had to do was to find Room 813. The door opposite the elevator had the number 828 on it . . . and the one next to that read 827. Slowly, methodically, Wally made his way down the hallway, reading the numbers on each door. Finally, he reached Room 813.

Stopping for several seconds in front of the pale blue door, he suddenly felt at a loss as to what to do next. He was so tired, and he needed sleep so very much. Soon, however, he again became aware of the object in his left hand, and once more he remembered the girl waiting for the package inside the room.

He tapped lightly on the door. His only thoughts now were that his mission was almost over, and that soon he could lie down in a bed and sleep.

"Paul?" a woman's surprised voice called from inside. "You're early, darling. Just a minute. Let me get out of the bathroom."

Early? Wally didn't know what the woman was talking about. As far as he was concerned, he was on time. If anything, he might be a minute or two late. But certainly he wasn't early.

"I'm coming, darling." Her voice sounded nearer this time.

A second later, the door opened and Wally saw a good-looking young woman in a white cotton dress standing in front of him. She looked as if she were going to a dance or a party, but instead of appearing happy, she looked startled.

"Oh . . . I thought you were someone else," she said. "I think you must have the wrong room."

But the sign on the door said 813. Wally was sure he had the right room, just as he had been sure that he was not early. Perhaps, if he held up the package, she'd understand. Something was obviously the matter, because instead of taking the package, the woman started to close the door in his face.

She mustn't do that, Wally thought. It was against the rules. The rules said that she had to accept the package. If she didn't understand the rules, he would have to make her understand. The rules were very important and had to be followed. He thrust his shoulder against the door to keep her from locking him outside.

"No, I told you! You have the wrong room!" the woman insisted as she tried to get the door closed. "You can't come in here. Please!"

"I've got something for you," was all Wally could say as his greater strength forced the door open again.

"But I'm not expecting anything. Please! Just go away! You're looking for someone else!"

Wally was sure she was mistaken. He wedged his body half inside the room, determined to get the package to her.

"Please! Get out of my room!" the woman kept repeating.

"It's for you. You have to take it!"

"No! No!"

But it was too late, because Wally was now inside the room and had closed the door behind him.

"Why don't you want it?" he asked, offering her the package once more.

"Get out of here! Get out!" She was screaming now and backing up against the dresser.

"Take it!" Wally said, stepping toward her at the same time.

"No! No! Please!"

"You have to! Take it! Open it up!"

He still couldn't understand why she was making such a fuss. Her screams were starting to get to him. Somehow, they didn't fit in with all the rules he had been following this evening.

"Open it," he repeated, now thrusting the package at the terrified woman's stomach. "And look, I gotta ask you to cut out that racket."

But still she didn't understand. Not only did she refuse the package, she batted it with her fist and caused it to fall on the floor. Wally bent down and picked it up, wishing all the while that she would stop screaming. He wasn't sure how much longer he could stand the noise.

"Take it, goddammit!" he shouted, frantically beginning to unwrap the package himself.

If she wouldn't open it, he would do it for her. There had been no rule about that. The rule had simply been that he couldn't leave until the package was opened and she had seen what was inside. That would be easy, too, since he now had her cornered between the dresser and the bed. He could make her look at it—and then he could leave. If only she would stop screaming. Why couldn't she just take the thing and let him get some sleep? Couldn't she see how tired he was? And why was she speaking some kind of Arabic dialect now? And barking like some goddamned dog? Why was she making it so rough for him?

It was even worse when he finally managed to get the paper off and remove the lid. Lifting the cover from the plain white box was like detonating a terrible explosion. The explosion didn't come from inside the box . . . it came from the frightened woman. At first, she uttered no sound at all. At first she only stared at the contents of the box in silent horror, but what followed was a series of screams so loud, so piercing, that Wally knew that all the rules in the world couldn't keep him from doing what he now had to do.

"Please, please," he begged, as his hands grasped her shoulders. "Don't do that! Don't scream!"

She wouldn't stop. "Oh, please, no!" she wailed, as he forced her down onto the bed. "Not again!"

Wally no longer heard her words as he took her soft neck in his hands and started squeezing it.

The craziest part was that he hadn't done anything so terrible . . . just delivered a box with a pretty red flower inside.

"I put him in one of the consulting rooms, Dr. Manning," Marge Kaplan said, indicating a closed door at the far end of the emergency room.

"Any problems?" Paul asked, as he and the nurse made their way through the crowded patient holding area.

"No, he seemed pretty calm," Marge replied. "He said he had talked to you, and that you were on your way here. I wasn't sure whether to believe him or not, but after that performance we had with him last month, I thought I'd better put him somewhere off by himself."

"Good," Paul said nervously.

"Paul, what is it? What's wrong?" Marge asked, sensing his anxiety.

"I'm not quite sure yet. I've got to talk to the boy first."

"Well, Doctor, we're here if you need us."

"Thanks, Marge," Paul replied as he slowly opened the door to the small, airless room where Wally Darrow was sitting on a folding chair. He closed the door quietly and walked over to the rigid young man.

"Wally, it's me," Paul said, lightly putting his hand on his shoulder. "How are you?"

Wally looked up at his doctor with the eyes of a helpless child. Without speaking, he grasped Paul's free hand and drew it to his cheek.

"It's all right," Paul said soothingly. "I'm here now. Everything's going to be all right."

Wally grasped Paul's hand even tighter.

"I fucked up tonight, Doc. I think I fucked up real bad this time."

"How, Wally? Tell me." Paul withdrew his hand from Wally's grip and sat down opposite him in another folding chair.

"I don't know what happened. Ever since I left your office, it was like I was in a daze. It wasn't until she was dead that I came out of it."

Paul nodded in a way that suggested he understood exactly what Wally was saying.

"Tell me more."

"There's no more to tell. I mean, there I was in this room with my hands around this girl's neck—and she was dead. Shit, Doc, I wasn't even drinking!"

Paul drew a deep breath.

"Wally," he said slowly, "are you saying that you think you did it? Do you think you killed her?"

"Who the fuck else could have done it?" Wally shouted hysterically. "That's why you gotta help me, Doc. You gotta convince them that it wasn't my fault. Even if I did do it, it wasn't me. It was somebody else, or something else . . . something I didn't have anything to do with. You'll tell them that, Doc, won't you?"

Paul stood up and tried to comfort his patient by patting him on the back. "Wally, Wally, trust me. I'm going to do all I can to help you."

"Oh, please, Doc. You gotta. I don't want to go to fucking jail."

"You won't go to jail, Wally. I'll make sure of that."

"What are you gonna do, Doc?"

"You just told me that, even if you did kill this girl, it wasn't you. I believe that, Wally, because I know you. I probably know you better than anybody else in the world knows you, and I know that you are incapable of committing a murder like the one you've described."

"But will they understand?"

"Of course they will. I'm your doctor. I've been treating you. I know your history. Even if they don't believe you, they'll believe me."

Tears streamed down Wally's face. "Oh, Christ, Doc. I knew you'd help me. I knew you wouldn't let me down."

Again he reached up and took Paul's hand. This time, he pulled it to his lips and started to kiss it.

"No!" Paul said, yanking his hand away. "Not here . . . they wouldn't understand."

Before Wally could say anything, Paul had left the room. The next thing Wally knew, he heard a click in the door. It sounded like a key being turned. But he was no longer afraid. Paul had promised to help him. That was all that mattered.

Outside in the ER, Paul walked swiftly to Marge Kaplan's desk, where she was busy filling out an admissions form.

"Stop whatever you're doing, Marge," Paul said urgently.

"What is it?" the nurse asked, looking up and noticing that Paul was even more on edge than he had been five minutes ago.

"We've got a lot to do. And we've got to do it fast. First of all, I want to get the Darrow kid out of the ER and into the Quiet Room."

"Really? He's that bad? He seemed so much calmer to me this time."

"Marge," Paul said in a low, confidential voice, "that kid just told me that he murdered his girlfriend a half hour ago."

Marge looked stunned.

"I don't know if it's true or not," Paul continued, "but I don't want to take any chances. So round up a couple of orderlies and a security guard. You'll need all the help you can find, because I don't think he'll take too well to being put in the Quiet Room again. Meanwhile, I'll call the police and get them over here."

"My God, Paul," she said. "I just had no idea."

"Neither did I," Paul said gravely. "But I should have known this would happen."

"Why do you say that?"

"Because in a way, I feel responsible, Marge. I had him in session earlier this evening. He was going on about this girl he had started seeing recently. Evidently, she didn't want to go out with him anymore because of his drinking. He made a couple of vague threats, but I didn't take them seriously. He'd made them before. I should never have let him leave my office in the shape he was in. I should have realized he was homicidal."

"Paul, you mustn't blame yourself," Marge said sympathetically. "I'm sure you did all that you could. Let's face it, with all the wackos we deal with, you just never know."

"I tried, Marge. I tried so hard. The shame is that I thought this kid was really getting somewhere." Paul shook his head dramatically. "You know, it's wrong of us to try to play God. We're human, Marge. We make mistakes."

"I'd better start taking care of things," the nurse said as she hurried away from her desk and motioned to a security guard.

When Paul was sure that she had the situation well in hand, he picked up the phone and dialed the police. He deliberately positioned himself so that he was facing away from the consulting room. He much preferred the image of Wally Darrow kissing his hand to that of his being dragged across the ER in a straitjacket. Paul's only hope, as he asked to speak to the homicide division, was that Wally would go quietly, but he realized that that was a lot to expect.

"Lieutenant Warren," a voice at the other end of the line answered.

"Hello, lieutenant," Paul said calmly. "This is Dr. Manning at New York General. I'm calling about the murder of a young woman at the Stafford Hotel on West Forty-seventh Street tonight . . ."

As Paul continued to recount his version of the story, he took great pleasure in the fine actor he was becoming. In the background, he could hear Wally Darrow's chilling screams, but they barely detracted from his pleasure and, mercifully, they didn't last very long.

August 5

The exhilaration of flight. At 40,000 feet, it's as though another dimension has opened up to me. More than ever, I realize that I must record all my thoughts, my observations, my revelations! So much was lost in the destruction of the first volume. Now I must make sure that my words are never destroyed again.

Looking forward to Greece—and to seeing Vivian. How I wish I could share it all with her—but afraid I won't be able to do that. To Vivian, indeed to the whole world, I must continue to appear to be the same Dr. Paul Manning that I've always been.

At breakfast with Alec Graham yesterday, I pulled off my Dr. Manning act quite well. Which is fitting, since he now assures me that I will be made department chairman once I return from Greece.

Even when we discussed HIS death, I was completely self-assured. Even when Graham told me about a woman who saw someone going down the stairs next to HIS room that night. A dark-haired man in his twenties! I told Graham that this description fits every Puerto Rican orderly at New York General. Ultimately, we decided to call a complete halt to the "investigation." Just too little to go on.

Fortunately, only a few of us know about any of this. Graham, myself, Hobson, Dr. Zimmer, and the woman Graham questioned. Graham was wise enough not to get the police involved. So we left it that he would talk to Zimmer, and I would take care of Hobson and the young woman. Hobson was very understanding. As for the young woman . . .

The only sad thing is the Darrow kid. Of course, it's his family I really feel sorry for. But at least the fact that Wally hanged himself in his cell will save them the agony and publicity of a trial. In a lot of ways, Wally's suicide is the one noble thing he did in his whole life.

Still, it's sad. The end of a life is always sad. But should it be? When so many people are better off dead than in life? The poor girl Wally murdered is another case in point. Considering the evil that possessed her for so long, I am certain that she is better off now. The reality of the situation is that two people in desperate need of salvation have been saved. I saved them. Just because Wally and that girl didn't understand why their lives had to end doesn't make their deaths any less right or just.

Sometimes death can be the ultimate solution. The radical cure. The true miracle. Perhaps of all my discoveries in the last weeks, this is the greatest. But my discoveries are only beginning. That's what's so exciting. There's still so much more to learn and so much more to be done.

My miracles have only just begun.

If you have enjoyed this book and would like to receive details of other Walker Mystery-Suspense novels, please write for your free subscription to:

Crime After Crime Newsletter
Walker and Company
720 Fifth Avenue
New York NY 10010